Forbidden

By Charlotte Stein

Forbidden
Intrusion

Forbidden

AN UNDER THE SKIN NOVEL

CHARLOTTE STEIN

red

AVON
IMPULSE

An Imprint of HarperCollins Publishers

Excerpt from *Holding Holly* copyright © 2014 by Julie Revell Benjamin.

Excerpt from *It's a Wonderful Fireman* copyright © 2014 by Jennifer Bernard.

Excerpt from *Once Upon a Highland Christmas* copyright © 2014 by Lecia Cotton Cornwall.

Excerpt from *Running Hot* copyright © 2014 by HelenKay Dimon.

Excerpt from *Sinful Rewards 1* copyright © 2014 by Cynthia Sax.

Excerpt from *Return to Clan Sinclair* copyright © 2014 by Karen Ranney LLC.

Excerpt from *Return of the Bad Girl* copyright © 2014 by Codi Gary.

EPub Edition JANUARY 2015 ISBN: 9780062365101

Print Edition ISBN: 9780062365118

AM 10 9 8 7 6 5 4 3 2 1

For my Crow

Chapter One

I DON'T KNOW how long I've been up here this time. Feels like days, but it can't possibly be. If it was days I would have peed myself. I would have made a mess or else starved to death, yet somehow I don't even feel hungry. Though really is that any kind of surprise? My stomach is churning and churning at the thought of what might happen soon. Every time it comes into my head all of this sickness rises inside me, and only the idea of having to lie here with puke stinking me up puts a stop to it.

The room is rancid enough as it is. Momma shut the windows ages ago, and the heat is making me sweat. I can see it shining on my bare arms and taste it salt-sharp on my upper lip, and whenever I wriggle I get a wave of that familiar smell. The one I never used to get when I was young and innocent, but now get all the time.

I scrub and scrub and plaster my body in deodorant, but it doesn't seem to matter. The ripe scent of my own body is still there, like a reminder of what makes Momma hate me now.

Not that I need any kind of reminder, what with the ropes around my wrists and ankles and the fact that I've been here forever. Or the way she looks at me when she comes in to see if I'm contrite and ready to plead for forgiveness. Of course I always tell her I am, but whether I do or not don't matter.

How can you really get absolution for being possessed by the devil? I could say ten thousand Hail Marys and recite the Bible backward, and it wouldn't make no difference. The demon she sees in me is invisible, and never seems to do nothing, so it's not like I can just scrub him out or act like he's not there. I can't stop spinning the room around like in that movie with the girl who has no eyebrows.

The room has never spun around.

You ask me—if I am possessed, I got some raw kind of deal. Seems unfair to have to lie here and be so severely punished, when I don't even get special powers. As far as I know I haven't so much as spoken in tongues or bent over in some kind of weird way, and for darn sure my eyes have never turned black.

So why do I have to suffer?

She says it's because I sinned, but I swear to God I haven't said or done a single damned thing. Apart from right then, thinking *damned*. But I know the devil doesn't jump into you for saying that. Most people don't even think of it as a curse anymore. The girls I used to go to school with said all kinds of things, like the one with the

F and the one with *S* and even worse—that one I'm not even going to give a letter to.

But none of them ever had the devil eat her soul alive.

And none of them had to wait all tied up in her bedroom, while some awful Priest comes to exorcise the evil spirits out of them.

I can hear him now, climbing up the stairs. He sounds like judgment day coming to greet me, footsteps as heavy as the hooves of the devil I'm supposed to be possessed by. Each one slower than the last, until I have to hold my breath or else pass out from the tension. Why isn't he racing up here? How come he's dragging his feet like this?

Because he wants to torment me before this has even begun, I think, and then all this water starts leaking out of my eyes. I pull at the ropes and wish for hands as small as mice just so I could get free. Though if I'm going to be wishing I'll try for wings, because Lord I want to fly away from here.

If I weren't tied I'd jump right out the window, wings or not. I'd suffer two broken legs and a snapped neck, if it meant I didn't have to face whatever awful thing he's going to do to me. Beat me, most likely, because Momma would never get anyone who wasn't going to beat me. He's going to stripe me from here to tomorrow—which I could take.

It's the other stuff that worries me more.

The boiling holy water and the drowning and the branding with crosses. She says he'll do that, all of that, and I believe her so completely I make myself bleed. My wrists are bleeding and my ankles are bleeding and I'm crying when the doorknob starts to turn. I scream for someone to deliver me from this hell, and just as I do the door swings wide.

He comes in, and after that I don't know what to think.

I go silent straight away, but not because I'm choked with fear. I would be if he was the image in my head— seven feet tall and old as sin, with eyes like winter at the ends of the earth. Then I'd be scared and screaming still. But he's not that way at all.

He looks like some ordinary man.

He ain't even wearing the robes and the collar and that. He has on this old beaten leather jacket—one that is far too hot for the weather here, if his flushed face is anything to go by—and even more astonishing a pair of jeans. I swear to God he's wearing jeans like he just did some fancy thing that jeans-wearing people do.

And he is *young*.

He's so young I don't even realize what's going on at first. I'm too busy gawking at his black, black hair and his lack of an angry beard and his kind of smooth everything. He steps forward and I marvel at how vigorous he is—not heavy and lumbering at all. And when he reaches for the rope around my right wrist, all I can do is look and look at his nice hands.

They're big, but they're not the least bit wrinkled or riddled with veins. He could be just a few years older than me—maybe twenty-five? He could be younger, even though that seems crazy. Momma would never bring someone like this to deal with me. She would laugh at someone like this. She took us away from the church because the new Priest was all young and into love and forgiving, so this makes no sense.

And then I realize what he's doing, and it makes even less sense than that.

He's untying me. He's doing it fast too—like he knows Momma might come in any second and stop him. Only I can see Momma in the door with her face all pinched and her hands wringing and wringing and she doesn't take a single step toward him, so maybe his quickness is something else.

It seems like he's horrified about something.

I think the horrified something might be me. He mutters a word as he sets me loose, and I'm pretty sure the word is *barbaric*. But him believing that and not wanting to thrash the devil out of me is so not what I've been thinking all this time that it kind of won't sink in. I keep trying to look around him to Momma, waiting for her to step in.

Or for him to change his mind. Maybe this is all just a trick or a trap, and suddenly he'll get out a switch to line my skin. Could be he has something worse on him—like a thick leather belt or some kind of whupping device— and I can feel my body bracing for it. Hurt like a son of a b-i-t-c-h when Momma went at me with that rolling pin one time, so Lord only knows what will happen with this man wielding something bigger.

He comes closer and I wince away from it.

Only I'm wincing away from nothing at all. He doesn't lash me or strike my face. He gets his hand underneath my bare bruised legs and the other around my back and then he says, "Put your arms around my neck."

Takes me a while to understand what he means, though. I sit there thinking—*this must be some other new kind of punishment*, and the minute I do as he asks, pain will make me pass out. He might have shockers behind his ears or something like it, and even after I find out he doesn't I'm wondering.

I wonder right up until he lifts me into his arms.

After which my thoughts go kind of still and stunned. No one has ever lifted me up before. Could be my dad did once, but I can barely remember him. And Momma sure never—she would have hated touching me this much. She would have complained about me making her hands all dirty, yet somehow the Priest don't seem to care.

He holds me all firm against his good clean clothes— that leather smells like old books and the shirt underneath just the same. And when Momma moans and asks what he's doing in a weak sort of voice, he answers like it's only sensible.

"I'm taking your daughter to the hospital," he says, even though it must be miles to Sacred Heart and I will have to go all the way in his car in my worn thin housedress and my stink of a too-hot room and my red hair so lank it looks black.

People will laugh at him, I reckon.

Yet he doesn't seem to care at all.

He doesn't even care when Momma goes to bar his way. He tells her, "Step aside, Mrs. Emerson," and for a second I go hot and cold thinking of someone disobeying her and provoking her wrath. Then I remember: he isn't just someone. He's a man of God and he has all the things she believes in on his side, and no amount of hand-wringing can change that.

She has to do as he says, and she does. She lets him go on through and down the stairs with me in his arms, though it's only once we're outside that I really feel what's happened. The breezy autumn air hits my fevered skin and I breathe out for the first time in years.

The breathing out sounds kind of like a sob. It comes out loud at any rate—so loud I know he must hear it for what it is. But if he does, he gives no sign. He just keeps on walking to his car, while I look back over at the clapboard place I lived in all these years. Somehow I understand that I'm not ever coming back to it.

This is it now, this is my freedom, and it looks like a Priest in his old sedan, with my momma running out in her black skirts calling to me. "Dorothy," she screams, "Dorothy," and in my head I'm already turning into someone else. They will ask at the hospital and I will say.

My name is Dot.

Chapter Two

THE BEST THING about the hospital is how cool and clean everything is. They put me in this nice blue bed with curtains around it, and all I can smell is soap or shampoo or something else as sweet as spring rain. It reminds me of that time Momma couldn't get a stain out with the homemade cleaner, so we went to the store and got stuff in a squirty bottle.

Smelt so good I put it on my wrists and behind my ears thinking it was perfume, and only learned different when the normal kids made fun of me. I didn't mind though. I would have rather stayed there with them chanting *toilet girl* at me down the halls than get the home schooling I got after that.

At home I never knew what might happen next, or because of what. Sneeze wrong and it's time for praying, and praying was almost never what other people do. I seen them in books and TV shows, getting down on their hands and knees and looking all happy about it.

You're not supposed to be whipped. You're not supposed to be drowned in a tub. I get that—and so do all the doctors. One of them takes me to this quiet room and uses a machine to look at my insides—which isn't half as bad as it sounds—and then once he's got the pictures he says to me real grave:

"Have you ever been properly treated for any broken bones?"

Of course I know why he asks. He can probably see my right wrist and how weird it is inside. It seems bumpy when you just look at it with your natural eyes, so it's got to be a whole heap worse underneath that X-ray thing.

He doesn't make me feel bad about it though. He just notes something down on his clipboard when I nod even though I'm completely lying, and leaves me to this kindly nurse who takes care of my bloody wrists. She squirts stuff on them and cleans them, and all while asking me about where I'm from so I won't think about it too much.

Then she wraps everything up in these bandages as soft and white as snow, and twice as good against my skin. I could sleep on a big heap of material like that. I could make a dress way better than any I left behind. I end up admiring them the way fancy ladies admire their bracelets, and only stop when it occurs to me.

All this has got to be costing. It has to be costing a ton. I bet this bed on its own is worth a thousand dollars, because I know I'd pay that much just to sit on it. The only problem is I don't have a thousand dollars, and I got no clue how I'm going to tell the nice Priest that. He might think because we live in that big house that we've got money.

Only we don't. And I definitely don't if I'm here now on my own. I suppose I could pawn my cross, but God knows what he'll think about that. He already looks real mad when he comes in to see me. His jaw is tight and his eyebrows are just about the angriest things I've ever seen—or at least, I think so at first.

Then I realize that this is just how they are. They're as black as his hair, as black as midnight, as black as my momma's skirts, and twice as thick as any I've seen on anyone else. I have to force myself not to stare at them, and not just because of the size.

No, mainly I have to force myself because those eyebrows look so damned good. They make his eyes seem so blue—like the ocean in some faraway place where everything is peaceful. And his skin almost glows around the edges of all that darkness, as pale and smooth as milk. Makes my own arms and face look darned near muddy by comparison, despite how little time I spend in the sun. I stay indoors so much he and I should be twins, and when I see we're not I kind of want to cover up.

I think about getting under the sheets. I think about pulling them all the way up over my head, like a dead person. And when I do it suddenly hits me what the real problem is. I get in this blinding flash of awful:

I feel this way because I ain't attractive.

But he definitely is. He's just about the most attractive man I've ever seen up close. He looks like one of them fellas in that magazine about cars and perfumes, and the only way I know he's different is that when he talks he says good things. He says kind things. He says godly things because he's a Priest and I just thought handsome thoughts about him.

"How are you feeling now, Dot?" he asks, and I go all weird inside. Mainly because I probably am a heathen monster who thinks about her Priest's eyebrows, but also down to the fact that he called me Dot. He asked me in the car what I wanted to be called and I said that and he just goes ahead and uses it no problems.

It's really no wonder I feel this way. Anyone probably would, after being rescued and asked and looked at with what I now recognize as concern. His eyebrows threw me off at first. My inexperience with anything like it threw me off.

But I get it now.

I get that I have a silly girl crush on someone, just because I'm not used to being saved. And in a second, he's gonna know it. Of course he will—he spoke seventeen hours ago and I still haven't answered. If I don't do it soon he might start thinking I'm brain damaged or deaf or some other thing the doctor tests didn't pick up on.

So I go with something simple.

"Yeah, I'm feeling real nice."

Only then he keeps talking. He keeps on at me. I suppose this is supposed to be that thing called a conversation, but he should really know that I got no clue how to do that. The longest I ever spoke to someone was a telemarketer who got the wrong number.

Plus I can't look at him while we do it. I know you're meant to but I just can't. His face was starting to burn my eyes. I can feel myself blushing already, even though I barely accepted his handsomeness and am completely aware why it's affecting me. He probably isn't even handsome at all to people he hasn't just saved. He's probably as ugly as sin.

I just wish his words were ugly too, so I could carry on thinking he's gross even when I'm not looking. But then he says:

"Everything is paid for here, so you don't have to worry."

And now that's all shot to s-h-i-t. He's probably a mind reader too, on top of being godly and good-looking and kind. If I lean in close he most likely smells of that cleaner only better, and then he shifts and this little cloud of man-scent wafts over to me and I just throw up my hands, I do.

"Thank you," I say, only it comes out sounding like something else.

Love, most likely. Love love love like some ten-year-old idiot.

"There's no need to thank me," he says, but there is.

I need to thank him for being so everything.

"Well, I want to anyway. For helping me."

"I could never have left you in such a terrible situation," he says, and I like that for two reasons. The first is that he doesn't tell me it was his godly duty, like I expect. And the second is that when we're talking properly I can hear an accent.

Underneath the Boston is some other thing.

A faint hint here and there, like wind chimes catching the breeze. It makes me turn my head without meaning to. Giddiness just gets the better of me.

"Are you from Ireland?" I ask, and though I reckon he wants to keep talking about the terrible thing, I can see the question had an effect. Those big eyebrows part. The corner of his mouth almost curls up. 'Course I got no clue why—could be he just likes being asked that.

Could be my smile is so big it's kind of catching.

"I am—originally that is."

"What's it like over there?"

"Are you wanting the tourist version or the reality?"

"The reality. Always the reality."

"Cold and wet and miserable," he says, and he does it in a way that tells me I should be disappointed. He expects me to be, I think. He spreads his hands and his mouth squinches sideways all regretful, so I know exactly how I'm supposed to react. I'm definitely not meant to lean forward before the words are out, eyes too bright and smile too wide.

And I shouldn't sound breathless when I say this:

"I bet it rains all the time."

I mean, what kind of person gets excited about rain? Only weird ones who spent most of their lives trapped in boiling-hot bedrooms, under skies that are constantly and depressingly dry. Normal girls would most likely shake their heads sadly or express dignified regret, then change the subject to something better. They would get an answer instead of a mystified silence—one I'm sure is going to turn into laughter.

Only it doesn't. Not even a little bit; not even at all.

After a second of this odd considering, he says *constantly*, in a tone I barely understand or recognize but like all the same. It sounds like someone sinking into a warm bath—which somehow makes it very easy to keep going.

"And the rain is freezing."

"You could die just standing out in it."

"Tell me about the sky—what color is the sky?"

"As gray as an old man's face and twice as miserable," he says, and then just like that I see what the tone was. I get it what this is. I can hear it even more clearly in his voice now, and even if I didn't the words he's using tell me what I need to know.

He likes talking this way. That was relief or relaxation in his voice, as though the angry, concerned Priestly part of him was getting heavy and it feels good to put it down. His shoulders were getting tired, I reckon, in some of the same ways mine were. I don't want to talk about the terrible things anymore.

I want to talk about this.

"Oh, that sounds so good. I bet you have to wear twenty sweaters all the time."

"We do—but we tend to call them *jumpers*."

"That only makes it cooler. Describe the jumpers to me."

"They're so thick you could stick your arm through one and not reach the other side. You have to use knitting needles as big as trucks to make them, and people often burn alive just from putting one on," he says, and the strangest thing happens when he does.

This sound comes out of me.

This *laughing* kind of sound.

Not that I would know for sure, seeing as how I haven't done it in so long. I even feel kind of self-conscious about it after it comes out, and maybe try to apologize a little bit.

But he stops me before I can. He waves his hand.

"I'm glad you're laughing. Now I feel okay about saying something so weird," he says, and then I think it's my turn to sink into the warm bath. Suddenly I'm halfway down the bed, eyes so heavy I can hardly keep them open.

I want to, though. Just long enough to hear him tell me more things. I've waited my whole life for more things, and want to gather them all up before they go away. He might be gone when I wake up. He might have other things to attend to, so I should make the most of this. Make the most of him—this Priest who has no thunder in his voice and no anger at me in his manner and all of these oddly comforting words about far-off places.

"Keep going. I like it," I say, and he does.

He describes what bread made from potatoes tastes like when covered in butter, while I slowly sink down and down and down despite all of my best efforts. I fight the weights on my eyelids and pinch my arm so I can keep listening, but of course none of it works. Right when I want to stay awake, someone makes me feel so safe that all I can do is sleep.

I WAKE UP gasping, half-sure my hands are still tied. Partly because of the bandages around my wrists, I think. But mostly because Momma is still with me. The second

I regain some kind of sense I want to get the hell out of there, and especially after I see that the Priest is gone. He went without even saying good-bye, and so now here I am on my own. Nothing to stop anyone from coming for me.

Nothing to stop anyone from forcing me back. Could I say no, if I saw her standing there in the doorway? I want to say I could, but I got no clue really. Not when my heart is hammering like this and my head is all foggy. Not when I can still taste the edges of my dream, full of fire and brimstone.

I just gotta get out of here—so much so that I barely stop to think about the silly plastic slippers they put on my feet or the fact that I have no jacket and no money and no place to go. I simply walk right out from behind the curtain and take the first turn I see.

No one tries to stop me. The place is so quiet it kind of sets my teeth on edge, every shadow seeming twelve miles deep and things ticking oddly behind every closed door. Feels kind of like a monster might jump out at me at any moment. I see a curtain stir courtesy of some non-existent breeze then want to break into a run, and only don't because of him. I just suddenly come across him standing in the dimness by a vending machine, and my whole body grinds to a halt. In fact the only thing that doesn't stop is my heart, which decides to jolt against something inside me the second I make him out.

Partly from fear, I think.

Mostly because he is still here. He never went away at all—he stayed. And he hardly even makes me feel bad

about wanting to go, neither. He says, "You want to come and sit down for a while before you go wherever it is you're going, Dot?"

As though I am completely allowed to leave if I want to.

But maybe it might be best if I take a break and think things through first.

So I do. I choose the plastic chair next to him by the vending machine, just to see if he is the same as he was when I went to sleep. He could have changed in the night, I suppose. Made himself more Priestly, perhaps. Got a Bible from somewhere to preach at me with, or called Momma to say that he has changed his mind.

All of which sounds like nonsense, I know.

But it only becomes otherwise when he talks again.

He waits until I'm settled, then says:

"I think the vending machine is cursed."

"Cursed by what?"

"The ghost of bad coffee past."

"There is no such ghost," I say, but I'm laughing when I do.

Mostly because I know he has me now. No way am I going anywhere, in the middle of a conversation about coffee ghosts. No way am I going anywhere when he is this person: the sort who does this on purpose to set me at ease. I might be only a fool girl, but I know kindness when I see it. I feel it warming me right to the bone, even as we go on with this weird conversation about all the wrong things.

We should be talking about Momma and what she did.

But boy am I ever glad that we don't.

"You wouldn't be saying that if you tasted this," he says.

And I just follow right along, full of gratitude.

"I wouldn't taste it at all. I hate coffee."

"What do you like then? Hot chocolate?"

"I want to say yes but that seems kind of childish."

"I thought the same and now look where I am. Drinking coffee cursed by ghosts."

"Let me try it. I will tell you if there is a ghost in it."

"I think we should just get the hot chocolate instead."

"The coffee is bad. What are the chances the hot chocolate will be better?"

"At least it will have sugar to take away the taste of ghost poop," he says, at which point I just got to ask. Or maybe not ask, but at least find out *something*. He just talked about ghost poop. He's just about the nicest person I ever met. I need to make it clear to him, even if I can't quite frame it as a question. "You know you're not like a Priest at all," I try.

And I'm glad I do. He takes no offense to it.

How can he, when this is his answer?

"Maybe because I'm not one—not yet at least."

Though I still have to confirm.

I still want to know for sure.

"But you have all the vows and rules and things to keep to?"

"We're expected to live the life we're preparing for, if that's what you mean. Our Father Superior is rigorous and exacting."

"So I still call you *Father*, then."

"Killian might be better," he says, and I get this weird feeling when he does. This kind of shivering thing, only on the inside and completely inappropriate. It shouldn't matter to me that he ain't really a Priest. And it definitely shouldn't matter that I get to call him by that name. I mean, what kind of person reacts like that to something so simple?

Most people probably find it ordinary, like Bob or Jim or Dave. Most people won't run their tongue all over those rolling syllables, thrilling over every single one. And most people definitely respond quick enough that no one mistakes excitement for something else.

"I'm three months away from the real deal though, just in case you're disappointed."

"Why would I be disappointed?"

"I don't know. You didn't seem disappointed that Ireland is a freezing nightmare covered in blazing-hot jumpers."

"Not even a little bit. I think that's what I was hoping," I say, and though I try not to make it sound like I mean anything else, I think it kind of does. I think it seems like I want him to be a different person. Not bound by vows or religion, but only the man who came to see me and talk to me. After all, if he is, then I get to like his eyebrows and his lovely voice. I can enjoy the fact that he's kind of weird.

And I can definitely say yes when he asks me what he does next, without worrying why I want to. Oh, when he asks, more than anything I want to.

"Would you like to come back to Boston with me, Dot?" he says, and my answer about bursts from my body.

I have to stop and rein it back in, because Lord knows what he might think if I let the real thing out. He might imagine I want to come for bad reasons, like sex stuff that he ain't ever going to suggest and I should not want.

After all, wanting is probably a sign of possession.

He might even be able to see it on my face.

Or hear it in my voice.

"So you can get a demon out of me?"

"I think you know there's no demon in you."

There might be, I think. If they come in small and make you think too much about eyebrows. Or hands. He has such good hands. They're so big and smooth I kind of want to slip one of mine into one of his, but if I do then this conversation might end.

He might not help me—and I need help.

"I can't pay you for anything. I've got no job or money or—"

"You don't have to pay. We have a program in my diocese for girls like you. A home run by the Sisters. You can stay there until you find your way."

"Does finding my way mean becoming a nun?"

"No, no, you don't have to be a nun. You can be anything you want."

I think of books. I think of buildings full of books and me in the middle of all of them, and television shows I can watch without asking, and people I can talk to without disapproving looks. I think of a brand-new life, just for me.

"When can we leave?" I say.

Chapter Three

HE TAKES ME to a store to get clothes first, but mostly all I can do is gawp at the fancy fashions and try to hide behind them when the saleslady comes over. She's wearing this dress with a diagonal zipper on the front and shoes made of two colors, and when she picks out a top to show me I see her nails.

They look about a foot long, and they got butterflies on them. Lord knows what kind of teeny-tiny brush made that happen. Or how much they must have cost. Even underpants are expensive in here, so nails like that have got to be worth a fortune. I catch myself staring at them and try to look elsewhere, but only wind up with a face full of the Priest.

I said no to too many things, so now he's just telling the lady that I want jeans and jerseys and a bunch of other stuff that I must have made eyes at, because somehow his guesses are all right. I did want that top with the purple cloud on the front. I do want those blue shoes with the straps across them. My own clothes look like worn old ghosts beside these things, and I'd be lying if I said I didn't want them.

It's just that he's paying for all of it. I ask him flat out as we're leaving the store—how am I ever going to repay you for all of this? But he just laughs and says:

"I think asking for something in return for a few bare essentials is called being a loan shark. Which I'm sure is a very nice profession, but it's not really what I'm into."

"What are you into then?" I ask, before I can stop myself. It just pops out as we get to loading the trunk with all my glamorous new stuff.

"Helping people. Being kind. You know—the tenants of being a Priest."

"Those are the tenants of being a Priest?"

I don't mean to sound surprised. It just kind of happens.

Luckily though he's not too rattled. I think he gets it.

I think he gets me, and all the things I have seen.

"Of course they are. I hope they are. What were you thinking they were?"

"Maybe something with fire and brimstone and lots of going to hell because you thought about what might be in the boy next door's pants," I say, then regret it right away.

It's just that he don't *make* me regret it.

Far from it. Real far from it. Crazily far from it.

"Well, that's no more me than drawing up a repayment plan would be. I don't mind if you want to think about things inside pants," he tells me, just as casual as someone talking about a summer breeze. He even goes about his business as he speaks, as though the whole thing is nothing. It must be something though, because the second he says it this thought just pops right into my head.

Even if the pants are yours, I think, and then want to die. He probably didn't even mean it the way it sounded. That's why he was so casual—he intended something else or I misheard. I twisted his words with my evil-demon-infected brain, and he's just now opening the driver's door to get at his bucket of holy water.

Or so I think, until I dare to get in next to him. I wait a while, half-afraid. But I don't need to be. Of course I don't need to be. He's not like any Priest I've ever known, and he proves it once I'm sat beside him. He turns to me with those eyes like twilight time and his black hair and one eyebrow always going up of its own accord and says:

"In fact, it's probably better you do so that nothing comes as a terrible disappointment."

I TRY NOT to think too much about the words he said. Whenever I do I feel weird inside, and not just because of his amused eyebrow. No one has ever said anything like that to me before. Not anybody—not even the ones who are supposed to be all open about sex and that kind of thing. Shelley Montague wore lipstick to school and short skirts and smoked in the bathrooms, but even she said that letting a boy do it to you made you a whore or worse. She said sex made you burn in hell.

But I know what Killian said is the opposite of that.

I'm pretty sure what he said is the opposite of that. He told me it was better to think of sex than not, which gives me good reason to imagine so. And then he added *disappointment* on the end, as though that was almost the worst thing that sex could ever be. Only the fact that he's almost a Priest makes me wonder if he really meant something else, because honestly how would he know? I bet he hardly has anything down there. I bet he's never had a sex thought in his whole life.

He's probably just trying to lure me in with pretend kindness and coffee ghosts before cursing me out for having racy thoughts.

Though if he is, he hides it real well. It's been three days so far and he *still* hasn't said a word to me about praying or getting on the right path. I keep looking at him without meaning to, and he never mentions it, not once. He don't even seem to mind when I start staring, though Lord knows I wish I could stop. A couple of times I try to close my eyes and think about other things, but I always wind up looking back at him.

It's the sideburns, I reckon. He has these long sideburns, as soft looking as down but somehow fierce looking too, and they keep drawing me in. And then there's his nose too, kind of big for his face in a way that should make him ugly.

It should, but it absolutely doesn't.

Nothing could make him ugly. Not even if he did bring eternal damnation down on my head for thinking about nice sideburns.

So the fact that he never does is a sweet thing indeed. In fact, he always seems to do the opposite. Halfway through some pretty, field-filled place, he asks me if I'd like something on the radio and I almost say no. I'm expecting hymns or prayers or that guy always going on about women fornicating then murdering babies. But instead he puts on the greatest thing I've ever heard in my whole life. It sounds like the wind if the wind was a song. It pours right out of his little doodad—you know the thing everyone has with all the songs on it—and I swear I fall in love right away.

With the music that is, not anything else.

Would be stupid to fall in love with anything else.

He's probably got women falling in love with him all the time, being all handsome and not talking about hell-fire and rescuing people and then putting on a man who sings to my insides. I can feel my soul fluttering when the man says *I want to run*. And then it gets to the part about *taking shelter* and *streets having no name* and suddenly my soul is doing more than soaring. It rushes right up against my rib cage and beats itself against the bars.

Makes me kind of afraid it's going to escape altogether—and not just because of how crazy that is. If my soul gets out, God only knows what it will do. I already can't stop looking at him, and that's when I'm in full control. Without me at the wheel something bad will surely happen, like my hand wanting to touch his hand. After a while he kind of drums on the steering wheel, and even though there are tons of things out the window that I should be interested in, that motion is hypnotizing me.

He has these real long fingers like a woman, and rings on them, too. Should really cancel out all the manly stuff about them, only it doesn't at all. They still look big and fierce. His knuckles are probably larger than my whole hands. Plus, that silver thing on his fourth finger down—I don't know if I would honestly call it girly. It looks like something a dog might wear as a collar.

Like a filthy punk, Momma would probably say.

But *filthy* and *punk* are the last things on my mind.

Touching him is currently at the forefront. Or at the very least talking to him about something. I try to remember how we started the conversations in the hospital, because once they got going it seemed so easy. We went back and forth so fast I can hardly believe it was me—which would probably explain why I can't seem to do it again. I open my mouth any number of times and nothing comes out. Everything I think of is silly or weird. If I ask him about the music I'll seem ignorant, because I don't know the singer and I don't know the song and I bet both are totally known by everybody.

And if I ask him about the jewelry I might look like some fool girl with a crush.

I already feel like some fool girl with a crush. Every time he looks at me I go all hot inside, despite all my best efforts to fight it. Everything he says is too cool or too kind or too great. He catches me eyeing a billboard that promises a million different kinds of ice cream at somewhere called Bob's Dessert Heaven, and just goes right ahead with an offer to stop. "Anytime you want to we can," he says, as though my feelings really matter.

No one has ever done anything that suggests my feelings really matter. It gives me this light sensation inside, the same way the music does. Eventually both of them are going to combine to send me right up to the clouds. I'm already floating close to the car ceiling—and that's before he suggests we stop off for the night. Somehow I was thinking we were going to sleep in here, considering how far away Boston is.

But no no no, he means a motel.

I'm gonna get to stay in a motel.

A room of my own with a bed that has a real mattress and probably a bathroom that might have a shower and oh my God a television set. Is there going to be a television set? I know the chances are good of there being one. Most likely I'll get to watch it, because even if he disapproves of heathen broadcasts he won't be there all the time with me. He'll go to bed in his own room and I can have the volume real low and then see all the movies and that one program with the spaceships in it, and Lord I'm so excited I make this really dumb mistake.

We get out of the car at this swanky-looking place called Marriott, with a big promise next to the door about all-day breakfasts and Internet and other stuff I've never had in my whole life, all these nice cars in the parking lot gleaming in the dimming light and a dozen windows lit up like some Christmas card, and then it just happens. My excitement suddenly bursts out of my chest, and before I can haul it back in it runs right down the length of my arm and all the way to my hand.

Which grabs hold of his, so tight it could never be mistaken for anything else.

'Course I *want* it to be mistaken for anything else, as soon as he looks at me. His eyes snap to my face like I poked him in the ribs with a rattler snake, and just in case I'm in any doubt, he glances down at the thing I'm doing. He sees me touching him as though he's not a nearly Priest and I'm not under his care, and instead we're just two people having some kind of happy honeymoon.

In a second we're going inside to have all the sex.

That's what it seems like—like a sex thing.

I can't even explain it away as just being friendly, because somehow it doesn't feel friendly at all. My palm has been laced with electricity, and it just shot ten thousand volts into him. His whole body has gone tense and so my body goes tense, but the worst part about it is:

For some ungodly reason he don't take his hand away.

Maybe he thinks if he does it will look bad, like an admission of a guilty thing that neither of us has done. Or at least that he hasn't done. He didn't ask to have his hand grabbed. His hand is totally innocent in all of this. My hand is the evil one. It keeps right on grasping him even after I told it to stop. I don't even care if it makes me look worse—*just let go* I think at it.

But the hand refuses.

It still has him in its evil clutches when we go inside the motel. My fingers are starting to sweat and the guy behind the counter is noticing, yet I can't seem to do a single thing about it. Could be we have to spend the rest of our lives like this, out of sheer terror of drawing any attention to the thing I have done.

Unless he's just carrying on because he thinks I'm scared of this place. Maybe he thinks I need comfort, in which case all of this might be okay. I am just this girl with her friendly good-looking Priest getting a hotel room in a real honest and platonic way so I can wash my lank hair and secretly watch television about spaceships.

Nothing is going to happen—a fact that I then communicate to the counter guy with my eyes. I don't know why I'm doing it, however. He don't know Killian is a Priest. He has no clue that I'm some beat-up kid who needs help and protection rather than sordid hand-holding. He probably thinks we're married just like I thought before, and the only thing that makes that idea kind of off is how I look in comparison.

I could pass for a stripe of beige paint next to him. In here his black hair is like someone took a slice out of the night sky. His cheekbones are so big and manly I could bludgeon the counter guy with them, and I'm liable to do it. He keeps staring, even after Killian says, "Two rooms, please." He's still staring as we go down this all-carpeted hallway, to the point where I have to ask.

"Why was he looking like that?" I whisper as Killian fits a key that is not really a key but a gosh darn credit card into a room door. So of course I'm looking at that when he answers me, and not his face.

But I wish I had been. I wish I'd seen his expression when he speaks, because when he speaks he says the single most startling thing I've ever heard in my whole life.

"He was looking because you're lovely."

Chapter Four

I TELL MYSELF he didn't mean it that way. He sounded kind of like his teeth were gritted when he said it, so maybe it was an angry thing. He was mad at the counter guy for checking out my chest or some such and he just softened the fact before reporting it to me. Yeah, that sounds right. The other thing—that I'm lovely or what have you—does not. Partly because I look like a dog's breakfast but mostly because if he meant it in *that* way, then he must have noticed. He noticed me the way I noticed him. He looks at my weird eye that is way higher than the other one and my crooked tooth and my non-existent upper lip and my devil hair and thinks, *Gosh she sure is delightful!*

When as any fool would know—one glance at my fat thighs is enough to put anyone off for life.

Plus, I stink. I stink like a horse's ass. My hair is so greasy you could fry an egg in it, despite all the cleaning

I got at the hospital. The second we get into my room I go into the bathroom, and I swear it's not just so I can escape the handhold of doom and the swell in my chest at the sound of him saying that thing I'm now never going to think about again.

It's so I can make myself presentable.

Only I can't, because the bathroom is something a wizard made. The faucets have no turning thing on them and even if they did I got no clue which is hot and which is cold. Neither of them has letters or colors on top. They're just these two ball things with a spout coming out the bottom, with this sink underneath that reminds me of the keys on a piano.

I'm kinda scared to go near it, truth be told. But the thing is, if I don't go near I'm never going to get clean. The shower in here is ten times worse than the basin. It has no dials and no head and the door makes a weird *shooming* noise when you open and close it. How on earth are you supposed to use a thing like that? Do you just stand in there and it comes on?

Is it like the spaceship program where you can speak and it obeys?

I don't know, and I feel weird about asking. Normal people are supposed to understand this stuff. If I go to reception and ask, all the people there will see how weird I am—so I guess it's a relief when Killian speaks to me through the bathroom door. A bit of a shock, considering I thought he had gone to his own room, but welcome, too. He don't care that I barely get all this.

He suspects I'm struggling anyhow.

"Are you all right in there, Dot?" he asks, so nice and polite I feel no shame about telling him what the problem is. The only embarrassment comes when he just does it so easy. I let him in and show him the crazy shower and he leans past me to turn it on. It only takes a wave of his hand and out comes the water, while my cheeks kind of heat a little.

Funny thing is though—so do his. He steps back away from me and his cheeks are all pink, even though it took nothing to do it and it ain't warm in here. Almost makes me think I'm mistaken, even though his pale face makes that impossible. When he blushes, you can really see it. It goes up high on his face and all the way down his neck, and it's only after he tells me he'll be on the other side of the door in case I need him that a reason starts to uncoil in my head.

He closes the door behind himself and then I glance down and see it:

Just before I approached the wash basin of doom I unbuttoned my shirt. I unbuttoned it *a lot*. You can almost make out my bra underneath—or you would be able to if I was wearing one. Instead there's just the curve of my bare breast swelling against the split in the material. I can see it when I glance up at myself in the mirror over the basin, sort of stunned and maybe appalled and okay yeah maybe this other feeling, too.

This hot feeling.

He saw me there.

An almost Priest and he saw most of my naked bosom. He went red because of it, even though he should be made of super-religious stone inside. He should be completely impervious to all mortal things, and the idea that he isn't is kinda jarring. It sticks in my head, like a burr would to the hem of my dress. I get in the shower just to shake it off, but all I can think when I'm in there is that I'm naked and he's right outside the door. If he walked in to check on me he'd most likely see everything.

Not that I want him to.

I swear I don't want him to.

I don't know why I go out into the main room in just the robe I find on the back of the door. If I had any sense I'd put all my clothes back on, because this thing is way too big and way too short and it keeps exposing me in places I don't mean it to. I take a step toward him and feel it slide off my shoulder. Another inch or too and he'd be looking at bare breast instead of just shoulder—though I reckon the shoulder is bad enough. I hurriedly pull the material back up, but I know he sees it.

The smile kinda dies on his face. He looks away again so fast his head would probably spin around if his neck wasn't there to stop it. And that blush comes back.

Lord in heaven that blush is something else. It twists my gut with guilty feelings, but it does some other thing, too. Wish I knew how to explain what this thing is. All I can say for sure is it brings up gooseflesh on my arms and makes my face go hot like his probably is.

Plus now I don't really want to sit down next to him, even though I get that it'll look weird if I don't. So I try to do it as far away as possible from him without looking like I'm doing that at all. I cross the room quickly, and take a seat as casually as I can. Then I cross my legs, just for good measure.

Only to have it backfire on me. The robe slides off my thigh when I move, so I end up perched on the corner of the bed like a gosh darn bird with my leg totally bare all the way past the knee. If he were to look down and to the right he'd no doubt see my birthmark, and my birthmark is so high up I don't even want to think about it right now. All I want to do is pull the robe closed, but that problem is getting in the way again.

That not-wanting-to-seem-like-we're-guilty-of-anything problem. Technically we haven't done a single thing wrong. He's not a bad person because my robe fell off my leg. I'm not a bad person because I put this thing on and came out here. We are just two innocent people staring at a blank, black TV screen in a deathly quiet motel room doing our best to not look at each other for even a second.

It's just a shame we're not very good at it. I dare to glance out the corner of one eye, and can see him straining so hard not to do the same. The muscles in his neck are practically vibrating. He keeps on staring straight ahead, but I can tell that's not where his focus is. His focus is on the periphery of his vision, and how much he can see without moving his eyes at all. I can almost make out the invisible barrier he's pushing against. Feel it standing in the way of what he wants to do.

When he suddenly speaks it's like a gunshot.

It breaks the spell all right, but by God it shocks. I nearly come right out of my skin, even though his voice is all faint and sort of trailing off.

"I just wanted to make sure you had everything you need, after your shower. In case maybe you didn't know how to work the TV or the coffee machine or needed to call room service. But if you don't need me then I should probably...I should go."

He glances at the door like the door is his Lord and Savior, those last words so quiet and fumbling they almost don't exist at all. Makes me wonder which it is—does he want to escape more than anything or want to stay so much that he can't really form the words? I think it might be the first one, but whether it is or not it don't matter. I'm too busy focusing on the one part of his speech that makes a little spark in me.

"You don't mind showing me how to work the TV?" I ask, far too breathlessly. I know it's far too breathlessly, because then he sounds even worse than he did before.

"Well I...I mean you really don't...I could but..." he stumbles out, while I rush to take it back. Quickly, before he condemns me to hell.

"Oh no, that's okay if I'm not supposed to."

"Not supposed to? No, no I just thought...it's getting late and...no of course you're supposed to. It's awful that you haven't been allowed before. Is that what you mean? That you haven't been allowed?"

"Well, one time there was this girl at school who had a square thing that you could watch on. But that was before Momma decided that I should be at home all the time in case I saw something bad or did something bad or decided to run away because I think she might have been a maniac."

"She was a maniac. There's no disputing that. So much so that if you ever want to do something about the things she did you—"

"No, I got no desire to do that at all. I just want to forget it."

"You can forget it. As long as you know she was definitely crazy and wrong."

"I know it. I do know it."

"I mean, the tying you up was a big clue, but even if it wasn't the fact that you just asked me if you're allowed to watch TV is."

"I was going to do it later with the sound down."

My explanation sounds so sheepish I wish I hadn't said it. He's going to laugh at me now, I reckon.

Only he doesn't at all. He doesn't even a little bit. He looks at me instead, for the first time since I came out of that bathroom. Not caring about my disobedient robe or my leg or anything at all other than gazing at me so fiercely it burns a hole right through my middle. It kind of looks like he might be about to tell me off in truth, but when he speaks it's anything but that. It's the opposite of that.

Has anyone in the world ever been so intense about the opposite of disapproval?

"You don't have to do it later with the sound down. You can watch anything you want, right now, completely in front of me. Just say what you'd like most and I'll put it on."

I really want to tell him here that I can hardly believe he's like this. That Priests should not be like this. That no one has ever been kinder to me than him. But I'm glad that eagerness gets the better of me. Greed just jumps right up my throat and leaps at that one cool idea: that I get to choose. That he prefers I do.

"I wish I knew what I'd like most. I guess one time there was this spaceship show—"

"Do you mean *Star Trek*?"

"It could be that I mean *Star Trek*. I'm kind if afraid to say though in case that's the most famous thing in the world and I'm the only one who doesn't know much about it."

"I really want to tell you that's not the case but…"

Man, I love the way his face goes when he says this.

Some of the fierceness leaves, but amusement replaces it. That one eyebrow goes up and his head dips a little—but the best part is that he ain't laughing at me. This is a joke we're sharing together, like in the hospital when we seemed to understand each other so fast and talk so quickly.

I don't know what it's called when people do that.

But I know I like it. I like that I can, so effortlessly.

"It totally is, right?"

"It's been going for like fifty years. You're actually the first person I've ever met who didn't know it was *Star Trek*," he says, then seems to realize how different that makes me. How different *he's* making me. "But you shouldn't feel weird about that—it's actually really…really…"

He's going to say the word. The one that says what this is.

Flirting, I think, *it's flirting*, so feverish I can't wait for him to get there.

"Actually really what?"

"I was going to say *cool*."

I deflate a little at that.

But only a little. And I'm already twenty thousand feet high and rising, so what does it matter in the end? When you've never spoken to anyone like this before, just getting to is its own reward. Just hearing him speak is putting me on the edge of my seat.

I'm practically squirming.

And I think maybe he is too, a little.

"So say it then," I suggest, and his shoulders go back. He shifts on the bed, hands clasping and unclasping, eyes searching for the answer.

"It seems awful to. It seems awful to be excited to show you things you've never seen before." He pauses then, like he knows he's gone too far or said the wrong thing. But I know why only when he finishes his thoughts on it. "I wish I hadn't said *excited* there. Pretend I used another word—like *interested*. Very mildly interested."

'Course, I immediately want to make it okay.

I just maybe go about it the wrong way.

"I would but *excitement* sounds much better," I tell him, aiming for sincerity and hitting Lord only knows what. Everything goes real quiet the second I say it—so much so I can kinda feel it in the air. It pushes at me like a heavy hand, getting stronger and stronger the longer I let it go on for. When I finally speak and explain, it's only because I can hardly breathe. I got to stop this just so I can get some oxygen in me.

"I mean I like the idea of you showing me," I say, only that's wrong, too. He tenses on hearing it and my face heats at the thought of how those words might sound if I was talking about something else, and then I rush on. "TV shows—I like the idea of you showing me TV shows. So if you want you could just put something on and then we could watch it together."

In a totally innocent way, I think, but don't add.

Adding it makes it seem like I don't mean it.

"I'll put something on. I'll find something," he says, in a manner that suggests he's grateful for the escape. Now he can focus on the television instead of me—and it works for a little while. He flicks through about a million channels, all of them so weird and different that I can't help exclaiming over them. There's one just about food and cooking even though that don't seem nearly enough to fill so many hours, and another with this documentary on it about how mermaids are real despite them not being at all. Some weird thing with guns that I think is a documentary too until he explains that people like to watch *crime procedurals*.

And then there is the craziest one of all of them.

The one he stops on, for no earthly reason I can think of. It must be the very opposite of anything a Priest would approve of, because it has monsters in it and people rejecting the cross and all kinds of oddness. Everyone wears these gigantic blouses, even though most of the cast are men. There is a ton of shooting just in the first couple of minutes, and as it goes on it slowly dawns on me that this is about vampires. I mean, the main guy sleeping in a coffin is a big clue. I read *Dracula* in the school library—I know all about that stuff. But mostly I know that there is no way I should be watching this.

And that I want to watch it more than anything.

I even think about putting a hand on his arm before he can turn it over. I note the channel number so I can put it on later when he's not here. He was kind enough to be cool about me watching television. But there have to be limits, right? There must be limits to his generosity, and vampires have got to be hitting that.

But I'm wrong, I'm wrong again.

"I used to watch this show as a kid," he says, right out of nothing. Just as the potato-faced guy is cursing out God for betraying him while wandering around in ladies' clothes.

I have to ask what he means.

"And then maybe you saw the error of your ways?"

"Hey, it's a good show. See, Nick Knight is the main—"

"Is that the potato-faced one?"

"That…yeah that might be him," he says, pausing in the middle to laugh.

"The guy who seems really upset with your boss."

"If vampires were real I'd probably feel a little more conflicted about it."

"How do you know they're not? TV just told us mermaids are."

He glances at me all suspicious—like he thinks I might be serious, maybe. Then when it dawns on him that I'm not, the suspicion turns into something else. A big mixture of stuff, made up of surprise and maybe some admiration.

"You're teasing me. I can't believe you're teasing me over *Forever Knight*."

"I'm really not, I swear I'm not," I say, even though I kind of am. It's just that I want him to carry on, and he might not if he thinks I'm being mean. "Tell me some more about it. Tell me why you like it."

"I don't know. I've never really thought about it."

"You must have. I know why I liked *Dracula*."

"You've read that? You were allowed?" he asks, and for just a moment I shrink away from the answer. I get that feeling of being bad or wrong somehow, before it fades into the knowledge of what kind of person he is. He watches this vampire show. He let me see it.

He gives me so much space to be me.

"I wasn't allowed. I did it sneaky like."

"So did I when I watched this."

"Maybe that's what you loved then."

"Being sneaky? Stolen moments?" he says, with that one eyebrow up and his eyes all lit with laughter. Makes me see him in his socks, creeping down the stairs in some Irish house that only exists in my imagination. In reality I bet they're just like our houses. I bet they don't really have gigantic fireplaces and Christmas lights always up and stone floors.

I think that's just something I read in Charles Dickens once.

"Yeah, exactly. Exactly that."

"Is that what you liked about it?"

"Maybe a little bit, sure. But other stuff, too."

"What sort of other stuff?"

I think of Lucy in her wedding dress. Lucy saying, "Come to me, Quincy, my arms long to embrace you."

Sometimes I wake up with those words on my lips—that's how strong they are in me. But of course I don't say anything like that. I keep it wrapped up tight.

"It's about girls who are punished for being different," I say, changing the word *sexual* for something vaguer at the last second. I think he knows what I mean though. His voice has an odd lightness to it when he next speaks, like he's trying to keep things innocent.

"That's an interesting interpretation."

"But it's right though, isn't it?"

"One hundred percent accurate," he says and then I know for sure. He understands I mean about the sex stuff in the book. He gets that same idea from it, buried underneath all the talk of unclean demons and chopping off of heads. Maybe that's even the reason he likes this thing, because a little while later when everything is almost relaxed and he's propped up against the headboard and I'm right there next to him getting grossed out by the blood and guts, he suddenly goes tense.

Then I see why:

The main guy is kissing the pretty girl. He has her face in his hands and their mouths are all open, everything so suddenly passionate that I find myself leaning forward. The room has gone deathly quiet like it did before and I can feel Killian next to me like a clenched fist, but I go to get a closer look anyway. I have to, because I think they might be using their tongues. Their actual tongues darting in and out of each other's mouths just like it said in that book Kate Waverley had, only somehow not half as awful as that sounded.

In fact I reckon it's not awful at all. It looks like they're really enjoying themselves, even though I know it's only acting. And there's something sorta engrossing about the whole business—a heat to it that I didn't bank on and so many noises I never thought kissing would make. All these soft sighs...how do they make those soft sighs with their lips moving everywhere like that?

They turn one way and then another way, as though keeping still is just not an option. If they keep still they won't get to taste every part of each other, or do this amazing-looking thing where one of them pulls at the lower lip of the other. Sounds gross I know but it's really not at all. Instead it makes me lean closer. It makes my heart turn into a galloping horse—and especially when her hand starts to move down to Lord only knows where. Is he going to do the stuff from page eighty-four of that book Kate had?

I think he might be about to do the stuff from page eighty-four.

I'm just about *dying* for him to do the stuff from page eighty-four.

So is it any wonder I react the way I do when Killian breaks the silence to say:

"I'd forgotten this part of the show. Maybe I should change the channel."

I swear I practically leap on him. I grab his arm and shout so loud I get all mortified a second later, but I can't regret doing any of it. The potato-faced man has just taken off his shirt, and I tell you what, he's much nicer there than he is in the general head area. He has muscles and the girl is touching his muscles and Lord have mercy on my soul it's just about the best thing I've ever seen.

Apart from maybe Killian's face when I dare to glance at him a second later, just to see what kind of damage I've done. Maybe check out how much trouble my immortal soul is in, even though I'm kinda starting to suspect the answer will always be zero with him. He don't think my soul is in trouble. He thinks I'm funny or strange or something else that makes his eyes go big and full of this odd wondering. His mouth is kind of open too, like I shocked him, but not in a bad way, I think.

And his words back that up.

"All right I won't, I won't," he tells me, so gentle and reassuring I nearly do something way worse than grabbing his wrist. He's sat with the arm closest to me kind of crooked, with this space underneath it. And I think about what it would be like to put myself there. If he would object to that, even though he didn't object to the hand I still got on him.

He just lets me keep it there all the way through the kissing scene—which turns out to be way less interesting than the soft skin on the back of his hand and the bone that juts out from just underneath his watch and most of all: the heavy sensation of his awareness. The pressure of his gaze as it tries to look and not look at my fingers wrapped loosely around him, and the idea that maybe he would say something if he thought it wouldn't make me go away.

Which sounds kinda crazy, I know.

It sounds so crazy I don't believe it at all.

Until he laces his fingers with mine, as the credits roll.

Chapter Five

I GUESS I know I'm dreaming. It's just that it's the weird thing where you can kinda control everything, but kinda can't at the same time, and everything feels super real even though it isn't. I ain't really on a cliff in Whitby in England. My guesses about what the real Whitby in England is like are as bad as my ideas about Ireland. In this fuzzy place between sleep and awake everything there is wild and dark, with these violent waves crashing against rocks made out of the glossy black stuff I know they have but also know isn't all over in this way.

This way is weird, like being inside a deep, dark cave. The only light comes from the moon, which is tons smaller than in real life and weak as water. It trickles down on everything in tiny amounts, hiding everything from me until the very last second. I don't even know I'm walking on bones until I've gone all the way to the edge of the cliff, though I don't exactly feel scared when I see it.

If I was scared I probably wouldn't stay there. I could make my dream legs run away or turn everything into some other place where no darkness is. I've done it before. I did it when Momma locked me in the closet under the stairs and I could barely sleep for nightmares about spiders. Here though I got no problem letting it go on as it is. I like the way my heart rattles in my chest. I like that slow, heavy sensation of being unable to get away from something dreadful.

It's coming in the boat I can see on the ocean. That big black boat that's probably nothing like the one Bram Stoker thought up, being as he was from olden times and this is more modern.

But then so is the Dracula who walks across the bones to me. I don't know how he got up here from the ship—flew I suppose, though most of me knows I'm just making it happen faster out of greed—and yet here he is all the same. Not in a cloak but a suit and no cape or chalky skin or widow's peak. His face is smooth and the color of moonlight, and when I turn my face up to his I see his eyes.

His eyes are what I expect, in some distant half-conscious way.

Not red, but blue. Blue and too familiar to me now—though I think my dream self tries to pretend he's somebody else. My dream self is embarrassed at how obvious I am, and I don't blame her. I should stop this, I know I should stop this. In a second things will go too far, then when I wake up it might be all I can think about. It might show on my face. My cheeks will go hot every time it creeps into my head, and after a while he's bound to notice. I can even imagine him saying, "What's the matter, Dot?"

At which point I'll most likely die of shame.

I'm dying now, but weirdly it don't feel that bad. It just feels hot and my stomach feels tight—only lowdown in this new place. This squirmy, heavy, syrupy sort of place that seems to swell upward to my nipples, making them stiff and achy. And it spreads down, down to that one good spot between my legs. The one I never touch with my hands and try not to think of too much but can't help thinking of here. He looks at me like he might do the touching, and then I just turn to water and wash away.

I don't even know he takes hold of me, considering my liquid state. I should gush through his hands or run right down his legs—only I don't. I don't at all. As a matter of fact I feel more solid in his arms than I ever have before back in reality when tingling isn't turning me into soup. I can make out every inch of my body, more alive than it has ever been. The blood just about crashes through my veins. A drum beats between my legs. I can hardly wait for him to kiss me and don't want him to do it at the same time, and doubly so when he misses my mouth altogether.

He goes for my neck, and I know that means biting. That was what happened in the book—he bit them and then they turned into bad women who want sex all the time. I know what it means, so how come I'm not screaming? Why am I not trying to get out of this sticky mess of a dream? I should be screaming but somehow I'm not at all. I'm breathing hard and my heart is hammering and dimly I realize I'm squirming around on the bed.

But I don't wake up.

I let him put his warm wet mouth on my throat, so real I can feel every detail. I get the slide of his tongue against my skin and the sense of something sharp, and then this pulling sensation. God, the pulling sensation is so clear—dense and fierce like someone threading a needle and thread through my skin then slowly drawing it out. I want to cry out over it. I think I do cry out over it.

I'm just not sure if the crying is because of pain.

How can it be when my parts are now full of these hot, deep pulses and my stomach is all clenched and my nipples are two tiny points? All of those things say different. And they get worse as this goes on, until finally I think I might beg him to stop. Every bit of control I had in this dream just disappears, and I have to plead with him. "Please," I say, "No more. I can't take anymore," but all he does is just keep on and on for so long that something new starts to happen.

He goes to kiss other parts of me—ruder parts, if I'm being honest about it—and something just seems to snap. I see his red, red lips part around one of my taut little nipples, that tongue as slippery as sin and twice as good, and this overwhelming rush goes through me. Dimly I know it for what it is: an orgasm. But knowing isn't really the half of it.

Feeling is the thing.

The deep throb of it is like nothing else, first small and startled and then thicker, rolling up through me again and again to the point where I can hardly take it. I want to scream beneath the pressure of it or at least kick out, every muscle in me straining toward and away from this…this *thing*. This cord of electricity totally alive in me, snapping and crackling and wringing me dry. How can anyone take it? How does anyone ever take it? By the time it's done I'm delirious.

And not just in the dream. In reality, too.

In reality, where Killian is.

Lord help me, he's still in the room. Worse than that— he's on the bed and he's calling my name like I made some big fuss and oh no oh no his arms are around me. What have I done? What did I do in my sleep? He must have heard me at the very least but what did hear me say? I try to focus enough to see his expression, but all I can make out is an unfamiliar flickering darkness and the fuzzi-ness of sleep. He could be calling for God to expel Satan from me with his eyes for all I know.

Which only makes me panic more. I fight the bar of his arms around me, thinking of the closet and the scald-ing tub even though that's unfair. He didn't put me there. I reckon he wants to take me out, but in that moment I don't know it. Momma has left too deep a mark.

The *dream* has left too deep a mark.

When I finally focus I'm sure I can see red on his lips.

In the aftermath I even reach up to check. I lie there in the circle of his arms, breathing shaky and trembling all over, and lift my hand toward his face. 'Course when I do things start to go weird. Anyone would know they do. His breathing is shaky, too. He has this gleam of per-spiration on his forehead just beneath the fall of his black hair—like he's been wrestling with me for longer than I want to think about—and heat comes off him in thick waves. It swamps me. For a second I can't breathe.

Maybe I don't want to. If I do I could miss something, some sign of damnation, some hint of ideas he can't possibly be thinking. He's never gonna kiss me in a million years. That's not what he looks like now—though God how would I know? All I got is words from books about foggy or misty or heated eyes, like desiring someone is closer to a weather report than a feeling. He could be about to rain over Switzerland.

Or he could be about to do something terrible.

He even moves down a little way, like I seen people do in movies. Head tilting just a little bit, lips parting like he might be about to say something—only without any words coming out. And then just as I come close to closing the gap…so close it kind of feels as though I'm stepping off the edge of a cliff…so close I could die because of it…

He suddenly *launches* himself off the bed.

And *launch* is the right word, too. He couldn't have gone faster if I'd shot him from a gun. I'm only surprised he doesn't crash through the nearest wall, though the effect is pretty much the same. He seems to search himself for a second, like he might have injured something in the blast or a lost an item he sorely needs.

I suspect it might be his immortal soul.

I think I stole it when he wasn't looking—or at least that's how it feels. I did something bad and can never take it back. Now he knows for sure how rotten I am inside.

Chapter Six

I TRY NOT to think about the thing that happened. Whenever I do this big red feeling crashes down on me like nothing else in the world and then I have to kill myself internally a million times. Why did I try to kiss him? He wasn't going to kiss me.

He probably just had a crick in his neck, and for his trouble I made him crash through a wall. When he talks to me now his voice sounds funny and he almost never meets my gaze, and I know all of that is my fault. I went too far—first with the unbuttoned shirt and then with the hand on his wrist and now with the worst one of all.

I just wish I knew how to make it better again. Other people probably know exactly what to say to make light of something like that, but all I got is pathetic fluttery comments about breakfast food and a feeling of doom whenever I catch him looking at me. I glance up over the menu at a place called Happy Pancakes, and see his eyes all full of this weird light.

But the strange thing is—I don't think the light is anger.

How can it be, when halfway through our sad, silent breakfast he does something so soft and unexpected I kind of flinch. I see his hand reaching across the table and think of stinging slaps and a fist in my hair, so ready to duck his punishment for my transgressions I almost do it. My whole body stiffens and shrinks simultaneously. That one time she dragged me up the stairs by my ponytail damn near sings in my head.

And then he touches a gentle finger to my cheek—as light as air and twice as hesitant, just brushing me there in a way I should find familiar but never could—and I realize. I get it about a second before he sees my reaction and explains.

"You had syrup on your face."

'Course I immediately want to laugh. I probably would, if other feelings weren't so busy getting in the way. My heart seems to have swelled to seven times the normal size. Tears are actually pricking my eyes—though Lord only knows why. I made a mess and he wiped it up. There is nothing tender about it.

I just keep making things that way.

And now I really have to stop.

I got to make things normal again somehow. The only problem is, every time I try I fail completely. Things start off fine, but then they just seem to descend into intense staring and double meanings without me even doing anything. I say to him:

"I guess I look like a total disaster, huh?"

Which sounds to me like the most innocent thing in the world. Only it isn't at all. In the middle of it there are traps I swear I didn't design, and he just falls right into the middle of one. "You never look like a total disaster," he says, then seems to realize what that might suggest. That I look like the opposite of a disaster. That I look neat and well put together and maybe even something else— something like that thing he said the other night.

The one he now obviously regrets.

Why else would that flush be spreading up over his cheeks? Why else would he glance away and try to fix the first thing he said?

"I meant that you just look as though you deeply enjoy your food," he tells me, but that turns out wrong, too. I think he just hit that *deeply* too hard or too hoarsely, because it sounds almost sensuous. He has to clear his throat and start that again too, only this time he's even more flustered. He shakes his head as though he can't understand how this happening, and fumbles out a bunch of stuff that just makes things worse.

"And I enjoy that—I mean not in a—not like—I don't *watch* you eating."

Now all I can think is: he watches me eating.

He watches my tongue curl up to lick syrup off my upper lip, same way I always watch him. In fact, he does that very thing all the time. He's doing it now even though he finished his plate and wiped his mouth five minutes ago, like a nervous habit only fascinating in a way nervous habits are never supposed to be.

Pretty sure they're not meant to make you go all weak behind the knees. But his lips are just so soft and mean at the same time—a slash through the middle of some plump piece of fruit—and his tongue is so awesome at licking. The end of it is real pointed and wicked looking, and the little bit of wetness he always leaves behind glistens like fancy lip gloss.

How can I help it?

I wish I could help it.

If I did maybe things like this wouldn't keep happening—like when we get back on the road and the silence starts to stifle us and so he puts some music on again. He puts on that same singer with the voice like someone reaching for something always just out of reach, and at first I swear everything is okay. I enjoy the singing a normal amount. I contain all of those other soaring excited feelings, even though the words are all about moving in mysterious ways and the tune is so wriggly I should really be going out of my mind.

I even start to feel kind of confident about it.

And then he goes and decides to sing along.

I could just kill him for deciding to sing along. That guitar buzz is bad enough. The guy coming out of the stereo is even worse. But Killian outdoes all of that and then adds some other junk right on top. He just suddenly bursts out with it, so loud and so insanely good I think I feel it punch me in the chest. I turn the second he does it, despite all my efforts to look at everything but him. I was busy counting the number of crazy billboards, but that goes directly out the window when he makes those sounds.

He should not be able to make those sounds. It seems criminal that someone like him is allowed to. He should have a boring voice that puts everyone to sleep or makes them think about climbing out of a window. Instead he has one that takes the word *hurt* and turns it into some other thing completely. I think his vocal cords are made out of sandpaper, and they rub that single syllable raw. I think there must be another person inside him who wants to sing so bad it claws out of his throat to do it.

And I cannot for the life of me stop staring at the attempt. I want to, because I can see him slowly starting to notice my enormous eyes on him. His voice dwindles and then dies as he realizes what he was doing, and it's just about the most painful thing I ever saw. More painful than watching my blistered hands peel. More painful than my bloodied knees.

So painful I should look away.

But I still keep on. I think I might be unable to do anything else—not even when he thinks he should explain somehow because my gaze is eating him alive.

"When I was younger I wanted to be a singer."

'Course this only deepens the mystery.

"What made you decide to be a Priest instead?"

"A lot of things. A lot of complicated things."

"I got time to hear them. But only if you want to, I mean. You don't have to. Momma used to say my curiosity was the thing that would eventually kill me."

"There's nothing wrong with your curiosity," he says, but I think he might be wrong about that. It sure seems to stab me somewhere, when he adds the rest. "Your curiosity is kind of the reason I really want to say. You just look at me with those eyes and some seam in me starts unravelling."

I mean, I suspected that all my staring was doing *something*.

But I had no idea it was this bad.

"That sounds terrible. I should stop doing that right away. Tell me what my eyes do so I can force them to be more normal."

"I like your eyes fine the way they are."

"Are you sure? Because I can put on sunglasses."

"That really isn't necessary," he says, so suddenly amused that I start to see it that way a little, too. Or at the very least, I manage to make it go that way.

"I could walk around with my hand over them at all times."

"I think that would cross the line from unnecessary all the way up to actively dangerous. The last thing I want is for you to fall down manholes because I feel like talking to you about my harrowing past," he says, and I think he intends it to still be funny.

He *intends* it, but that don't stop the hollow silence that follows.

Or the question I just got to ask.

"Your past is harrowing?"

"Well, no more than yours."

"That only makes it sound worse," I say, then sort of want to take it back. One of the things I like about him most is that he don't press me for details on any of that. He don't act like my counselor, talking me through the hard times. Now here I am trying to make him talk about his hard times, and I can see it makes him uncomfortable.

His hands tighten on the wheel.

His shoulders shrug around inside his jacket—like maybe it suddenly fits him poorly. Or is it his skin that suddenly doesn't sit right on him? Think it could be his skin.

"It was bad in a different way. No one ever tied me to a bed or broke my bones or made me feel filthy for perfectly natural feelings. But it made me want to stop people who did things like that. It's the reason I convinced Father Lucas to let me help you, instead of just leaving it to whoever your mother could persuade into doing things her way."

"I wondered why you came so far."

"He was against it. He wanted to come himself when I raised it but…"

"But what? Why did it have to be you?" I ask, and he pauses then.

Though said pause is so heavy he might as well be speaking anyway. I can hear the suggestion in him and see the conflict and can guess what the answer is even if he would rather not say. He may like this Father Lucas, but he don't trust him. Not to do this. And sure, the reason might be anything at all. Maybe he is old and tired and could never have made this journey. Maybe he would have handed me over to the hospital and had done with it. Maybe he's not quite as compassionate about things like this.

Or maybe something else.

Sure seems like it, when Killian finally speaks.

"It had to be me because I know what happens when someone really believes in demonic possession and tries to treat it with exorcism. Either you end up with justification of the abuse of a perfectly normal person, or true illnesses go completely untreated and someone dies—as my father did."

"Your father died because someone thought he was possessed?"

"Yes," he says, then seems to pause again.

This one's clearer, however. Much clearer.

Who would want to say, about something like this?

It hurts my heart just to hear it.

"He suffered from blackouts. You know—he would wander somewhere without knowing where he was going, wake up in a place he wasn't supposed to be. 'Round the village we lived in, people found it kind of funny. Or they did right up until the point it suddenly wasn't. He woke up one day with his own blood on his hands in a strange woman's bedroom, and from there things went downhill very fast," he says, and I think there that he will stop.

His knuckles have gone white now. His face is blank in a way it almost never is. Those eyebrows are always doing wicked things and his eyes are like doors in his head—or at least they were, until he has to tell me all of this.

And he does tell me all of it, too.

"It's funny, you always tell yourself that no one will ever do something so cruel and strange and superstitious, until you actually see it happen. Even when I came into your bedroom, I thought this would never be like it was

with my father. Times must have changed by now. And your mother just seemed a little eccentric. Not like she'd tie you to the bed. Yet here we are," he tells me, so weary I want to make a bed of myself for him to lie down in.

But instead I just have go with the next best thing.

"Here I am, safe with you," I say, so he knows for sure how special he is.

Somehow I don't think he does, though. He sounds too like he thinks the battle is already lost, when he finishes this little tale. "I wanted to be a different sort of Priest to that," he says. "One who helped people, and didn't let superstition cloud them, and served God as though he is love instead of hate."

So I try again. I make my voice strong, even though I can feel it trying to waver under the pressure of my tears. And I lean toward him—more toward him than I've ever dared before. I even put a hand on his arm, despite the way he stiffens over it.

And I keep it there, as I speak.

"I think you're all of those things."

"Even if I sometimes sing?"

"*Especially* because you sing," I say, thinking he will definitely hear me now.

And he does. He definitely does.

I think he hears me too *much*.

I got that hand on his arm and my voice is probably all full of passion or some such and so when he glances my way our eyes lock. They lock so hard I think he might be about to run right off the road. He stops off for gas just a couple of minutes later, and though he says a bunch of

reasons why he needs to, I think I know what the real one is.

It becomes clear when we get back in the car after bathroom breaks we didn't need and food buying that neither of us wants, and my seat belt gets all stuck on the way out. 'Course he immediately leans across to fix it. He gets a hold of the strap and pulls and twists, and then I shift a little just to help him. I swear I only do it to help him.

But whether I meant that or not the result is the same:

The back of his hand brushes something he should never be brushing. He knows he should never be brushing it. The moment it happens he jerks back as though my right breast burned him. He even makes a noise like that too—a cross between a sharp intake of breath and a startled grunt—but worse is the word he chokes out a second later. "Sorry," he says, "sorry," as though all of this is his fault when really it's mine. I'm the one with enormous ridiculous boobs that get in everybody's way. I was the one who moved into his hand.

I might even have done it intentionally, if anything Momma said about me is right. I could have the devil lurking in me, just waiting to make men fondle my chest. Too eager for the look of him and the feel of his hand in mine. Too wanton, too wicked, too greedy.

Or so I think, until he cuts me off.

"It was me, Killian it was me. I shouldn't have—" I start, and there is his voice, the one I imagine he might use for a sermon, the one that sounds like a Priest condemning his flock to hellfire from the pulpit, only not at

all not in the least. How can it be, when his words are the wrong way around?

"Stop right there," he says. "Do not say you shouldn't have. There is never anything you shouldn't have done. The way you move or the way you look or the things you say are all as sweet as a sunset, and if someone thinks about those things it has nothing to do with what you have done. People choose to do what they do, and they can choose not to. They can choose to be good and not be tempted to do anything, no matter how...no matter how hard that may be. Do you understand me?"

'Course I nod with all the vigor in the world and say yes in capital letters and all surrounded by gold. But the thing is: even though I do I really don't. The only thing that gets through those words is the way they make me feel—like my insides are swelling into something more beautiful and better than anything that came before—and the sound of the great and terrible hitch in his voice.

The one that stood between *no matter how* and *hard*, so thin a single push could make it break.

Chapter Seven

I THINK ABOUT that hitch between his words. I think about it so much my mind overflows and makes a mess all over the floor. I spend the next few nights in various motels somewhere around the midway point—seven hundred miles from Louisiana but with seven hundred still to go—pacing back and forth, torn between that crashing red feeling and the growing sense that there is something more going on than just me staring at him and wanting him.

If it was just me then he probably wouldn't keep saying good-bye so awkwardly at my door. He always seems trapped for a second between the kind of gesture he wants to make and the one he thinks he'd better do because things are weird. Usually he ends up with a clumsy hand-shake, but after a particularly long and hot and tensely silent day in the car something else happens. Nothing big, but then small is gigantic with us.

All he does is pat me on the shoulder, and that seems like too much. I can still feel it now, searing a hole through my body. Kind of afraid to take my clothes off in case I uncover a handprint burned into my skin. His hands are enormous so I could hardly miss it—though Lord knows I want to. I want to with such a fever that I go to sleep in my dress, just in case there really is something to see.

Not that it really helps me. I only end up dreaming about it instead, in a way that is still not appropriate for a woman and a nearly Priest. It seems it at first—nothing is sexy about falling into a big pit and being devoured by hell demons. Everything is just awful and nightmarish in a way that feels so real. I swear I can make out their cold breath on the back of my neck. They claw at my ankles and the sensation sizzles through to my actual body.

And when I scrabble at the sides of the pit and find no purchase, the frustration is too intense for me to take. I know I'm grinding my teeth back in reality. I know my legs are peddling and peddling, like some dog having dreams about a bone. I think I would do just about anything to get away—which maybe explains why I make him out of thin air.

One second I'm falling with no hope of ever getting free. The next his hands are on me. He reaches for me and I reach back and that's when things start to go real bad. That's when I end up rolling around with him on the ground, at first in a completely innocent way but then slightly less so. A lot less so. How much less so is suddenly having no clothes on?

I got no idea when that happens in the dream. I only know that everything shifts and his skin seems to be against my skin and oh it feels so good. So good I know I do something lewd, back there in reality, where everything is too heated and too tense.

I put a hand between my legs.

But the funny thing is—I don't worry about it nearly half as much as I did before. I barely feel any shame about the whole thing, in part because I know that Momma was wrong but also because of those words he said. The ones that made something swell inside me and still do now, despite the terrible thing I see when I open my eyes. In fact, the thing is so terrible for a second I think I must be dreaming.

He could barely say goodnight to me.

He *cannot* be in my room.

But he is all the same. I squeeze my nails into my fist and he stays right there, no more of an apparition than the chair or the TV is. If anything his presence is thicker, denser, like someone filled him with treacle before standing him there. His hair is so black spaceships probably get lost in it. His eyes are so dark I could almost believe they're not the least bit blue at all and never were from the first.

And the look on his face...

The look on his face will stay with me forever. Every muscle in there seems to be sagging, and all of his effort is going into holding them up. His eyebrows are straining under the pressure and his jaw is a clenched fist, and the reason for it is pretty clear. He must have seen me writhing around on the bed. He probably saw me putting my hands between my legs and moaning through the whole thing and oh I know I should feel mortified about that I know I should but God help me I don't.

Not even when he tries to explain.

"I heard you call out and thought I should see if you were okay," he says, and then I wait for embarrassment to wash over me. I wait but it never comes, and I know why. I can actually hear it in his voice. I can hear the lie, so bright it burns his words down to nothing. They turn to ash and blow away beneath the pressure of that one false-hood, and I disappear with them.

He knew when I called out it was not because of a nightmare.

He knew, *and yet he came in here anyway.* He heard me moaning like some animal in heat and came running, opened my door with a key I barely knew he had, and burst right in to see whatever I might have been doing. Then when he saw it, he stayed right where he was. He watched from that shadowy corner, in a way he can never now get out of.

Not even when he doubles down on the lie.

"I wanted to make you feel better," he says, which should really make him seem all caring. But somehow the words come out wrong. They sound rubbed raw and sort of rude, like his thoughts aren't full of chicken soup or soothing hugs. His thoughts are full of the other way of making someone better, to the point where I have to ask about them.

I have to know what the other way is.

"And how did you want to do that?" I ask, so eager I know it shows in my voice. I can hear how trembly I sound, even though I'm sure his answer is going to be tame.

I'm sure right up until the point where he says it.

"I could hold you in my arms," he tells me, and I swear it feels like he's already doing it. His voice is so full of high and tight I could never mistake it for anything but longing.

And I want him to know that I long for that, too.

"That sounds good, so good."

"Stroke your hair and your cheek."

"I think I would like that."

"Maybe whisper soothing things to you."

"Will you tell me what the things are?"

"I hardly know myself. I hardly dare think about them."

"Then maybe I should say instead," I say, but only because I'm damn near bursting with them. I can feel them pressing at my lips, like they've been held back so long they can hardly wait. No one would ever know we met for the first time a week ago.

It feels like a thousand years. I met him before in some other life—one better than this, with no obstacles in the way and no enormous pressure that makes him say:

"No, God in heaven, no please, let's just pretend a little longer."

I never heard anyone sound the way he does when he speaks those words. Never seen anyone look the way he does, either. If he had a pulpit in front of him I feel sure he would beat it with that one clenched fist. Pain has made a great furrow between his brows, so deep you could bury a body in there. I think he *has* buried a body in here.

I think it might be his own.

"That what I did was have a nightmare, just a nightmare," I say, but I don't make it a question. Questions are not as soothing as I want this to be. They leave cracks in things and I want the way forward to be smooth for him. I don't want him to dig more holes in his own face. That fist is so tightly squeezed together I'm afraid for the flesh inside.

And his voice that lovely voice that one I heard singing in the car…

It comes out in pieces now. Breathless and broken in two.

"Only that and nothing else. No other words about anything," he says, and I nod.

I try to smile for him, and tell him more things that will make this okay.

"Most likely best that we do. I have a feeling saying the other things might make me burn in eternal hellfires," I tell him, intending something lighthearted.

But I should have known—I should have guessed it wouldn't come out like that.

Maybe nothing between us ever will. Our time of jumpers and jokes is done.

"Oh, Dot, no, no, nothing is going to make you burn in eternal hellfires."

"How can you be sure? Seems like you think all of this is pretty wicked."

"Only for me. Only for me, Dot, never for you. Nothing is forbidden for you."

"Not even dreams about you taking all of my clothes off?" I ask, though I swear I only do it because I want to know for sure if what I feel is wrong. I don't mean to make his face sag the way it does, or turn his eyes so bright and dark. I don't mean to make him speechless, but somehow that's what I've done.

It takes him an age to answer me, and when he finally does his voice is faint and his gaze has gone far, far away from here.

"Not even that. Not even if it makes me look the way I probably look now."

"It looks like I'm killing you. Like I got a knife and stabbed you in the gut," I say, and now my voice is the thin and helpless thing. There are tears in it even though I swore I would never cry again about anything ever. I wanted to be strong from now on, but how can I be?

I did this to him. I did this horrible thing to him. He might say that none of it is my fault and that he is the one to blame, but I doubt I can ever really believe that.

Or at least, that's what I think until he speaks again.

"You could say nothing at all and that would still be the case. I've been bleeding since the moment I met you. The only difference is that right now I don't know how to hide it."

Neither of us says anything after that. Him because I reckon it took just about all his remaining strength to get it out, and me because shock stops up my mouth. 'Course I *thought* sometimes that he felt something for me. I knew that there were moments between us that sparked and crackled. I may be a naive girl but I'm not a fool—I saw and heard and felt.

But I guess I didn't really think it was anything.

Or that he would say it out loud. He said it *out loud*. He admitted it, Lord I never thought he would admit one tiny part of this. I see now that I imagined myself being taken somewhere then saying good-bye and him walking off relieved. I thought *I* would get to walk away relieved—only that can never happen now.

What relief can there be when we're already mortally wounded?

I have to know if there is some. He has to tell me.

"Then maybe we should pray. Pray to be delivered from this," I say, partly because I still believe that God is there and listening but mostly because I just don't know what else to try to bring him some comfort. Praying seems like the best idea all around.

But oh boy am I wrong about that.

He nods and walks to the bed like someone strolling through a dream. I get why though—as soon as he sits down I see that I miscalculated this. I pictured him making the sign of the cross over my head and asking the blessed virgin to make me a better person. In no way did I think he would have to be this near me.

That he would be on the bed with me, knees nearly touching mine. So close to my thigh I can feel it burning the air between us. Eyes like fire and lips parted and then oh no then he does the worst thing of all. He *takes hold of my hand*. He picks it right up off the bed, and then he *clasps it between his*.

Though as soon as he has I think he realizes it was a mistake. He might have thought at first that he was just wanting to pray with me like this, but I can see that he now knows it can never be that way. Any kind of touching between us, no matter how well-intentioned, is always going to feel like this—like we both got hold of a live wire while dipped in water.

But there's no going back now. If he goes back it would mean accepting that even praying is beyond us. Or that maybe it was never really what either of us intended.

I just secretly wanted him to sit close to me.

And he just wanted to hold my hands. He wanted to do it tight, tight, tight, with his big fingers laced together around my little ones and everything in the middle so hot and no one saying anything even though I know he should. The minutes tick by though and still he doesn't. He just looks down at the place where we're now joined, as though if he only searches hard enough the answer will be there. Some words will come.

And when they still don't, I begin for him.

"Maybe we could start by praying that I stop feeling lustful things," I say, but I can see just by the way he glances up at me that these are the wrong words.

He has so many better ones, so many lovely ones.

"Oh, Dot, I will never pray for that. I will never ask God that you stop being a normal woman, and you should never ask it either. Never think about that, not even for a second."

"Then what should I think about? What should I pray for to help be free of this?"

"I would ask that you find someone worthy of your attention and your desire. That you find someone who can give you all the things that you so sorely deserve because believe me, Dot, you deserve them. Lord knows if I had the power to give them to you I would," he says, and though I know he intends it to soothe me no soothing happens because of it.

The opposite happens. A fever happens, in my soul.

"What are they? What are the things I deserve?" I ask, because I am greedy. I am wrong and I am bad and I am so greedy, but I swear if I am then he is the same. He knows why I ask and yet he answers in kind.

"Someone to kiss you the way you should be kissed."

"Tell me how I should be kissed. Tell me how."

"Like your mouth is a sweet, ripe peach at the end of a journey across a barren and brutal desert. Like nothing could ever keep your mouth from his. Like he would burn down the world just to feel you in his arms and put his lips against yours," he says, and I know rationally that I asked for this. I know I did, but still it shakes me.

That he would speak it.

That he would mean it.

That he would keep on even though my heart is thundering so loud he must be able to hear it. My eyes feel like moons and my breathing is more like gasping, but he goes on.

Lord in heaven, does he go on.

"To put his lips all over your body," he says, and I want to stop asking him about it and urging him on but I can't. Not when his voice is suddenly different—so different that I'm starting to wonder. It sounds like he only wants to pray, on the surface.

But underneath…

"All over? All over everything?" I ask.

And he *answers* me.

That's the thing.

He answers.

"Everywhere. Not an inch of skin left untouched. No place overlooked or forbidden," he says, and that suspicion burrows a little deeper. It gets right under my skin, forcing me to keep pressing on even though I feel sure this must be the limit.

"Say what the places are," I say, part of me sure he will refuse this time.

Then thrilling to the depths of my soul when he doesn't.

"The curve of your collarbone, and the sweet softness of the inside of your arms. All down your back and then oh then…" he says, and I don't know what gets ahold of me harder. The fact that he said *oh* the exact same way I might, as soft as air against skin and twice as breathless sounding, or the fact that he left it all trailing like that.

He has to know that letting it go like that puts me on the edge of my seat. That it makes my heart thump long and slow and my body want to lean toward him, just about dying for more. My voice sounds so desperate when I whisper to him, so full of desire I can barely keep it in check.

"Yes then…" I say, so close to that edge now I can feel air under most of my body, so near to him I just know he can tell I'm trembling. Anticipation has made me a caged beast, just waiting and waiting to see if he will turn the key and set me free.

And when he does, when he says those three words—*between your thighs*—everything just bursts out of me. Everything just bursts out of him. "Yes oh yes please," I tell him, and he responds in kind. He gives me more, as though he had a cage all of his own and once I am let loose then so is he. Now he can tell me about slow, wet kisses.

Only the kisses are not on the mouth.

Lord in heaven, they are not on the mouth.

He *tells* me that they are not on the mouth.

"All over your spread sex," he says, as though *spread* and *sex* are two things he is totally allowed to talk about. Never heard no one in my entire life say them aloud, and I didn't think the first time would be from him.

Though it isn't just the words.

It's the heaviness of his gaze, pressing down on me. The way he licks his upper lip when he says it, as though wanting a taste of what that would be like physically. Really, it's no wonder my next words come out as a moan. Or that they make no sense.

"Oh Lord, Lord let me," I say, even though I got no clue what I want him to let me do.

Something to relieve this ache inside me, most probably.

Something that stops his every filthy word from feeling so good.

"Until his mouth is slick from it."

"Yes let me yes."

"Until your body is trembling from it."

"And his hands, are his hands—"

"His hands are all over you. His hands can't get enough of you. They might be by his sides or on the wheel of his car. They could be clasped in prayer or folded in his lap. But know always that they would rather be on you," he says, and that's pretty much the final straw for me. He must mean himself. It must be okay to say more and do more.

I might die if I don't.

I have no choice but to try to meet him in kind.

"Does he know the same of me?"

"He does now. He does now."

"He knows that I dream of sinking my hands up to the wrists in his hair and spend hours imagining the heat of his bare back against my palm. He knows that I want to touch him all over in the same way I swear I want to do it all the same," I babble, but still he holds back a little. He keeps that pronoun distant.

"Sometimes he thinks of nothing but."

"Of my hands on him."

"Yes, that."

"Of my body against his and my mouth all over him kissing and kissing down to that hard thing between his legs, to that stiffness, just waiting for something soft and wet around it," I say, and now I think he will do it.

But it still shocks me when he does.

"God forgive me, yes."

I hear that *me* instead of *him* and that hiss in his final word, and my heart lurches against my breastbone. There is nothing left to do after that but give in. He's going to give in. I can even see him leaning toward me, head tilted at the perfect angle for a kiss. His lips are now so close I could poke out my tongue and taste them. Just a little bit more and then—

"Forgive me, and allow me to stay true to the path I have chosen. Give me the strength to help this woman and not break my covenant with her and with you. Dear God, let her have the peace she deserves, from this day forward," he says.

Before dropping my hands like they suddenly burn, and stepping off the bed and back toward the door. No kiss, no relief for that ache, only this:

"Amen."

Chapter Eight

WE DRIVE THE rest of the way in silence, only it doesn't really feel like silence at all. Seems to me that we're both talking loud as can be—so loud it makes the air vibrate between us—but without actually being able to make out any of the words. Probably for the best though that we can't. I'm willing to bet that his would be mostly prayers and mine would be mostly apologies, and none of that feels like a good note to end on. I want him to keep being my friend, but that can never happen if we ever talk again about the incident.

Or the other incidents.

Or maybe just the whole trip. Yeah better that we never discuss the entire trip, because to be honest even thinking about it makes me go all weird. I get that hot tingly feeling again and my face burns and the urge to do something about it builds up way too high.

So I keep silent. Even when he pulls up outside this ugly red building on some dirty gray street, and turns to me with this tense look on his face, and says we should probably not see each other again for a while, I keep silent. The only thing I do is nod, when he says, "Or at least we should only see each other if you need me, as a counselor or a Priest or as support."

Though Lord knows I want to do more. Desperate words suddenly beat against my teeth. I have to press my lips so hard together they bruise just to stop them getting out, and my hands want to do all sorts of mad things the second he gets out of the car. They almost grab ahold of him and haul him back. The only thing that keeps them from doing it is the thought of a thousand Priestly eyes staring down from that red eye of a building, and even then it's a close thing.

So they see me grabbing, I think.

Better that than never seeing him again.

How in heaven am I supposed to never see him again? I barely want to stop seeing him now, with him not three feet from me. The thought alone is lead in my stomach, and that's way before I get outside and discover exactly what Boston looks and feels and sounds like. Somehow I imagined a big church beside a pleasant park, but the closest I see to that is the machine across the street uprooting a tree that reminds me of a witch's fingernail. The courtyard that the home for girls and the library and the church are set around looks nothing like the idea of a courtyard in my head, and everything is loud, real loud and dirty and rusted looking.

Plus the rain doesn't smell like rain at all. It smells like iron filings.

All of this smells like iron filings.

And now I got to go through it alone. No one to exclaim at about anything. Nobody to ask for explanations. It was miracle enough that Killian turned out to be kind and good—the chances of everyone being that way have got to be slim, and they get slimmer when I see inside. The only noise is a grandfather clock slowly ticking in the corner, so you already feel like a big, loud intruder just by walking in the door. Then I get a look at the floor and that feeling gets worse.

The wood is so polished I can practically see my face in it. I gotta wonder how he dares to wear his boots all over that surface, because boy am I worried about my new sneakers. They're pretty clean, but I know for a solid fact that I stepped in a puddle on the way in. Seems likely I left dirty footprints in this house of holy help for girls, for which I reckon I might have to pay.

Can I not even ask him if I will have to pay?

I glance his way while we wait for some evil nun to probably punish me, but he refuses to look back.

Even though I know he can always feel me doing it. That flush is starting to creep up over his neck and his cheeks. By the time someone gets here he's gonna be bright red. He might even give us away—an idea that scares me so much more when I see the man come to greet us. His eyes are two pale stones set in a face like heavily lined metal, and they seem to look at me without really seeing. Like maybe there's another layer of something on top of my skin that no one else knows about.

No one else except for him.

Father Lucas, Killian introduces him as, and then I let myself be the tiniest bit relieved. This is the one who let him rescue me, which must make him okay. And when Killian introduces me, his great, still face cracks into a smile, so I think I might be safe thinking that. Lots of things tell me I should be, like the way he shakes my hand and the way he talks all soft and even and the way he asks an apple-cheeked woman to help me settle in. If he were as cold as he first looked he'd never want that to happen.

He would turn me away now, I think.

And yet. And yet. And yet.

That first look he gave me remains in my mind, long after everything else has faded. I lie on my narrow bed in a room with a sad-looking Jesus on the wall, everything so strange and new my thoughts should be full to the brim with it all. There is a girl in the room next to mine singing funny songs and outside my muddy window Boston thrums and *Killian* I want to think *Killian* and the kiss between my legs. But as I close my eyes there is only one thing tattooed on the inside of the lids:

Father Lucas, seeing the second skin that surrounds me.

THE ROUTINE IS real simple and safe feeling at Saint Agatha's, which makes it easy to sink right into. In the mornings us girls help out in a big bright silver kitchen to help starving people, and then we get time to ourselves to do as many things as we want, and then there are chores in the house to keep it nice and sometimes chores in Father Lucas's home down the street and the big old church too often needs polishing and looking after.

It all keeps you super busy.

So busy that pretty soon I think I will forget about everything that happened. Most of the time it feels like a fever dream anyway. Like my life before and my time with Killian is something I recently woke up from and should shake off as quick as possible. It was probably all just nonsense brought on by trauma anyhow. I am shell-shocked from it, Sister Marlena says, and I reckon she might be right. I was blown apart by my own life, and so naturally I liked the look of my savior.

In a little while I will see him as something else, as just a man who helped me, as a shoulder that I leaned on and now have to leave behind.

Or so I imagine. So I even begin to believe, as I go about my brand-new business day after day. I scrub floors and polish endless amounts of wood; watch show after show on the tiny TV in the couch-stuffed communal area; read all the books I can lay my hands on in the library that belongs to the church. I talk to girls my own age with problems much like mine—girls who flash gaps between their teeth caused by drunken rages when they smile and girls who got involved with drugs.

Girls who cry. Girls who scream at night. Girls who become my friends, somewhere in the middle of me turning into a real person. A whole person, who can make her own choices. I get a job working in the library, and in the spring, Sister Marlena says, I can start looking for my own place.

And if my heart speeds up when I one day hear that yearning voice on the radio, then it speeds up. If I catch myself singing it as I shelve books then so I sing. Don't mean a single thing. I swear on my everlasting soul that it never did. It was just a crush. It was just the trauma. It was just saving and being saved I know it I am certain of it I am sure.

I am so sure.

Until the fire.

I SMELL THE smoke first, though my head is too sleep stuffed to do anything about it. The dream I was having tells me that someone burnt a slice of toast. Momma left it going and in a second I will hear her cursing Satan for making the bread catch. My breakfast will be cinders and soot again while she eats the new batch. I can even taste it in my mouth.

And then I remember.

Momma is gone. She never even calls here or did anything to find me. For all I know she might be dead and in my dark moments I sure hope so. Could be that's why I'm lying here under a blanket of smoke in fact—because when I open my eyes that's what I see. This hovering mass of gray-like hell come here to punish me for wanting my mother to die. In my heart I'm still a sinner, even though Sister Marlena says sin is in your actions not your every waking thought.

She must be wrong, I think.

But honestly I only do it for a second. Just one second of weakness, then I rip back the covers. The rational side of me takes over—fed daily on a diet of culture and kindness and friendship until it grew strong—and I go for the door. I keep low and feel for heat and then run out into the hallway, now far less worried about my immortal soul and much more concerned that everything is so *quiet*. No one is racing around like me. The hall is full of smoke and I can hear that ravenous crackling fire sound from somewhere downstairs, but everyone is still in their beds.

They're all going to burn to death if I don't do something. Susie Polanski who always says her two names together and Trisha who smiles despite the teeth and Caitlin who told me stories about her boyfriend and the things that boyfriends do. I told her I had never felt anything for any man, but she could tell that I was lying. "It will be our secret," she said, and now she's going to die.

I cannot let her die. My eyes are streaming and my head already feels weird and heavy, but I refuse to let her die. I bang on her door until my knuckles split. I bang on everyone's doors, and holler their names just as loud as I can, and when no one responds I claw my way through the clouds of darkness to the end of the hall. There is a fire alarm thing somewhere there, I know there is. I see it every time I come up the stairs, bright red and obvious in the day but so much harder to find here.

It takes me far too long to get it.

But thank God by the time I do Susie is with me. I see her stumbling toward me, half in and half out of her robe, eyes streaming just like my own. "What's happening, what's happening," she moans, but I got no time for her to fall apart. I tell her straight—go right down and get Sister Marlena and Sister Mary up.

And then I smash the glass with my elbow. I pull the little lever down and brace myself for sirens that never come. Of course they never come. They should have been here way before now. The detectors should have picked up all this smoke, but somehow none of that has happened. They must be defective or else out of batteries, which just leaves me and the hammering and hollering.

Only problem is: now I'm as hoarse as anything and so woozy I can hardly raise my fist. Seems like a miracle when Caitlin emerges from her room, and even more of one that we manage together to get through Trisha's locked door. We just bash until it gives and then have to haul her out of bed, but we do it. We get her arms around our shoulders and make for the door, half-blind from the smoke and crashing into every damn thing. My hip cracks against the big old table in the hall and I stand on something that makes my foot scream at me, though by this point in the proceedings I barely care about minor pain.

The threat of the fire is the only thing to worry about. We have to almost go down the stairs sideways because of the heat and the height of it, reaching up over the left side of the staircase. And even then we can all feel it pushing at us. Within a second or so my face feels tight, like I sat out in the sun too long. Getting to the double doors out of here is the sweetest thing to ever happen to me, and especially when we burst through and find a torrential downpour.

I never been so glad to get rained on. I turn my face up to the sky and let it wash over me, before I do one single other thing. Only after my skin has been soothed and my lungs filled with great gulps of cold air do I start panicking about anything else—like Sister Marlena and Sister Mary and the cook who sometimes sleeps on-site and the people who might be in the buildings behind. Does anyone ever stay in the library? Could someone have been studying there, then fallen asleep?

A student, perhaps?

A particular student who never seems to come, but could have today. *He might have done today*, I think, though I tell myself some other story as I search the gathering crowd. I only want to count the people who were in my home with me. Who will have really been in danger. *No one and nothing else*, I think, and yet somehow I seem to be walking in a certain direction. Sirens are starting to flash not too far away, but I walk.

And then I run. I pick up speed before I even know where I'm going, down through the courtyard where I sit every lunchtime now and toward the library. But when I pass that silent building, I keep going. I keep going until I round the corner just beyond the seminary and see what I really wanted to all along.

The one I was really looking for.

I can tell myself all I want that I care nothing. But the second I see him a different tune sings inside me. I take in his clothes—just his pajamas as though he saw the smoke and ran right here from his dormitory in a blind panic. And I take in his burning gaze, and know that panic was only for me. It comes to me in a great rush, washing away all other thoughts and doubts. Suddenly I see it clear, as we stand here in the rain with barely five steps between us, both of us breathing too hard and staring too hard and knowing.

None of it was a dream.

It was as real as he is in front of me now. As real as that song now going in my head—the one that says over and over about giving yourself away until something inside me just breaks. I hear the crack of the seal over my feelings and then I simply have to cover that last bit of distance. I know it might be the wrong thing to do. I understand that he could stop me before I get too close.

But I can do nothing else.

I almost hurl myself into his arms, so hard it should take him off his feet.

If he were not there to catch me. If his arms did not reach out for me before I take a single step; if they did not surround me so tightly the second I get close. He holds me like he would sooner die than ever let me go again, and I do the same. I don't know how I ever did anything different. What made me think it would be okay to never see him again, when seeing him again feels like this? I might as well be drowning. I sure sound like I am. The cry that comes out of me when I finally have him in my arms is too loud and too desperate—but I get no chance to be embarrassed about it.

The sound he makes is the same.

Everything he does is the same as everything I want to do, right down to the hands suddenly in my hair and the look all over his face like his heart is breaking and burning all at the same time and the words he tries to form and fails. No words would be adequate, I think. Nothing could explain what this is, not even anything beginning with *L* and ending in *E*.

Only a kiss is enough.

The kiss I am sure he will never offer.

The kiss I am certain can never be.

And the one he gives me, right there in the light of Saint Agatha's, with the taste of smoke still in my mouth and the sirens wailing somewhere in the distance. His hand in my wet hair and his lips so hard against mine—like he wants to press it down into him forever and never forget. As though he wants to make the memory as brutal as possible, in order to keep it with him through the days to come.

I have no idea why, though.

This is never, ever going to be the only one.

Chapter Nine

I WANT TO pretend to everyone that nothing happened, but wanting to and doing are two real different things. I can feel the kiss showing on my face at all times, to the point where even the ambulance guy asks me how come I look dazed. It must be near morning by the time they are willing to let me go back to my business—and by business I mean normal stuff like checking to see if everyone is okay and hugging the Sisters when I see they are all right and going with them to the hotel we're going to stay in until everything is settled.

I definitely do not mean kissing Killian.

I might want it to happen again, but I still don't know if I see it as ordinary exactly. Like something I could just share with little Susie when she whispers that she's afraid of being in the Holiday Inn, rather than reassuring her that no maid is going to surprise her naked. Or a question

I could put to Father Lucas, when he stops by to see how we are.

Is it okay to kiss him again? I imagine myself saying, then almost want to laugh at the ridiculousness of an idea like that. Almost, but then I see his stone eyes skimming over me as though searching for something, and any urge like that dies down.

For just a second, I feel sure he knows.

He sits with me on this bench outside the hotel, and puts one hand over mine just briefly, and looks at me so intently I can feel it against my skin like a thumbprint, and I get this coldness inside. Maybe because his fingers are icy. Maybe because of something else—I don't know, I don't know. But I do know that when he says, "Anytime you would like to talk to me, you may come and do so," I am not in the least bit comforted.

Instead I sort of want to deny accusations he has never made—a notion that seems real silly once he walks away. Partly because it was just one kiss and nothing about me says it happened, but also because as I watch him go I notice something kind of at odds with the idea of him being this strict, cruel knower of all lies.

He has two odd shoes on. And not just odd shoes, neither—one is brown leather and the other is a gosh darn sneaker. No Priest who goes around wearing one sneaker can be all that bad, I reckon, even though the sight does stay with me. I think about it long after the whole thing, right after any ideas I have of kissing Killian again.

That one cold hand, I think.

And the odd shoes, as he walked away.

IT'S ALMOST TWO days later when I next see the man I kissed. Everything has almost gone right back to normal—heck, I'm even doing a real normal thing when I see him. Just here at my new job in the library putting books back on shelves. Minding that perfectly ordinary business I thought about earlier. Nothing sexy about any of this. Except for that intense look in his eyes.

Oh, he can say all he likes that he wanted to check if I was all right. He can tell me he should have come to see me sooner, to make this look like some long-overdue kind of thing. My mind still goes to the fire and the rain and the darkness, and the sound he made like some siren song in my head. The feel of his hand making a fist at my back; the hard press of his mouth against mine.

And I am made bold by all of it.

"I know that's not why you really came," I say, so low I have to take a step closer to help him hear. Or do I do it to make it easier to touch him? It could be, seeing as how my hand is there on his lapel before I know anything about it. My fingers curl around the material and tug just a little—though even a little must be too much. He looks at that hand like it might be on fire.

Then back to me with so much of something in his eyes. I want to call it pain. The lids are low and there's a line between his brows, all of which suggests this hurts him. That knife is still in his stomach, and right now I might be twisting it. Though if I am, his next move makes almost no sense at all.

"How do you know? How do you see me?" he says and then he just seems to dissolve down over me. The end of this bookshelf is barely a millimeter from his back and the main desk only another few steps from there but he gathers me into his arms.

"God help me," he says.

But I doubt God would be willing. Not after he kisses me, with that collar still around his neck and these high holy books at my back. I put one surprised hand out to steady myself, and feel their brittle spines beneath my fingertips. They dig into my shoulder blades when he turns me—or do I turn him? It gets kind of hard to tell when I'm in the middle of it all. Feels like I'm rolling around on the floor with someone while standing up. At one point our legs tangle together.

But it has to be done.

It seems like the only way to get close enough. To kiss him hard enough. One firm press is far too little for me, and I think it might be for him, too. It feels like it, when he puts his upper lip over my upper lip and his lower one somewhere in between and quite suddenly it occurs to me that this is the real thing. This is openmouthed like they do in the movies, only so much better than that ever looks. No one ever says how much it stings to feel a man's stubble against you, or how sweet that sting can be.

I never see anyone sigh over the heat, or the soft pulling sensation of it all, or the slick slide of him against me. Everyone just seems to take all this for granted, but everyone must be nuts. He must be nuts, because right when it starts to get really good—I get a hint of his tongue flickering in and just a touch of his teeth—he pulls away. More accurately, he *wrenches* himself away. He ends up stood on the other side of this space between the stacks, with a table in between us. And he puts his back to me, for good measure.

Though neither of those things appears to help.

He's still breathing hard a whole minute later.

The hand he puts through his hair is shaking.

His voice is shaking when he finally speaks.

"Maybe we should just talk for a second."

"What do you want to talk about?"

"The same things we did before."

"Kisses over every inch of my body then."

He turns at that, expression caught between shock and something else. Irritation, I think it is, because he knows I know what he meant. He wanted to go back when we had those rat-a-tat-tat conversations about TV and coffee and singing and things, and instead I go straight to what we ain't ever supposed to mention.

"That wasn't exactly what I had in mind."

"So tell me what I'm allowed to say."

"You know what I think of the word *allowed*."

"I know that you went away because I forgot what it meant."

"I went away because *I* forgot, not you. I still want to forget now," he says, and I come very close to wavering then. He said before that he wants to live his life by the principles even if the vows are not yet taken. He wants to be this and forget, and I should never stand in the way.

But then I think of the kiss.

More than that—way back when we prayed. I can no longer deny that he meant those things the way I thought he did. That part of it might have been just a crush, but if it was then he was in it with me, too. The knife is in us both, and when he says those words while looking at me that way it forces all kinds of things right out of my mouth.

Wicked things, I think.

Tempting things.

"Then do the forgetting. Or is it a sin to ask you to?"

"I think it might be a sin to carry on standing here."

"I got no direct connection like you, but I feel pretty sure God is okay with standing."

"Only if you keep your eyes to yourself while you do it."

"Are your eyes not keeping to themselves?"

"I feel as though they're trying to eat you alive."

"I don't mind though. I don't mind at all."

"Whether you do or not, *I* should mind. I should be able to look away, yet every time I try I feel some part of you calling me back. Some tiny thing that I am so sure I will forget forever if I stop drinking it in," he tells me, after which I can hardly help myself.

"Tell me about the tiny things. Tell me what they are," I say, so lustful sounding I should be ashamed.

But his answer makes sure I am not.

"The jutting bone at the edge of your right wrist. The crooked incisor I can always see just below the line of your upper lip. That light in your eyes always calling to me and the way it burns when I come. How can I not when you are as lovely as the sun on some December day? When my every thought is of you and every word you say?" he asks, as though he really expects me to answer.

He steals my breath with speeches like that, then imagines I can just carry on talking.

I have to tell him that I can't.

"I feel afraid to make any more now," I say, then wish I hadn't after all.

He thinks I mean something else. He thinks I mean that he should take it back.

"Pretend I never behaved so poorly," he says, while my heart grows a new beat in my chest just for him and my feet want to march to where he is and my every thought is of those things he said. Whatever he thinks of the way I talk, he is more than equal to it. I hardly even know how I manage to keep on. I want to swoon to the ground like some girl in a sexy book.

But I settle for bursting out words instead.

"It isn't the way you're behaving that scares my words away. It's the idea that the wrong ones might stop you from carrying on. I got no idea how or what it is I do that gets you to talk like that to me, but if I knew I would do it a thousand times over," I say, so fierce I have no idea how he might respond. Part of me imagines an appeal to be quieter.

None of me imagines what he does.

He crosses the distance between us, sudden enough that I almost step back. And then he just takes my face in his two hands and kisses me again like he never said nothing about not being supposed to. He kisses me as fiercely as my words just were, over and over again until I go boneless. I think the only things holding me up might be those hands, which makes him taking them away something of a problem.

I sag against the shelves the second he does.

And this time, I got no qualms about telling him to return to me. It was bad enough when he did that open-mouth thing and tangled his legs with mine. It was bad enough when he looked at me with those helpless eyes. But striding across this small space to kiss me like that is just too much. Every part of me feels hot and aching, like I pulled a muscle everywhere only awesome. My nipples are poking at my blouse, so tense and tight I can hardly move without making them tingle.

Saying something is a necessity.

"Do it again. Do it again and this time don't stop."

"What other choice do I have apart from stopping?"

"You could carry on until the end of time."

"Right now, here, in this place?" he asks as though I might say no.

I don't let him know how close I am to saying yes.

Only the sound of a page turning somewhere not so far away stops me.

"Anywhere would be okay. They put us in a hotel until the fire damage is repaired and you could come to me there and—"

"Please do not tell me what I could come to your hotel and do."

"Why not?" I ask, though I know.

Because it sounds seedy.

Because it's something a harlot would say.

Because it's greedy and wrong and bad.

Or at least it is until he answers.

"Because I might *do it*," he says, with far too much feeling for this quiet space. Up until this point we've been talking barely above a whisper. But these words come out strained. They have a big black line underneath them—a fact he seems insensible of until much too late. Now we have to freeze and listen and listen for that turn of the page, and when it comes he sighs with relief.

Then seems to reassess.

"We should just…we should sit down for a moment. Cool off a little," he says, which sounds good in theory I guess. But in practice it makes everything worse. The only chairs are on the same side of the table, and I can tell he don't want to move one of them. If he does it will say that he has no self-control or I am a temptress he can never be next to, and he seems reluctant to suggest either.

I wish it were otherwise though. Now I got to sit next to him in the state I'm in, so close our thighs have to touch. I can feel the seam of his jeans against my nearly bare leg, and beyond that all kinds of things I probably shouldn't think about. We're supposed to be cooling off. Not getting hotter and hotter because our legs are barely brushing under the table.

But that's what seems to be happening.

He asks me how I've been doing, working here, and though I answer him with cheery enthusiasm I feel certain my skin is starting to blister. All of this sweat is gathering in odd places on my body, to the point where I feel awkward and uncomfortable.

Every part of this is awkward and uncomfortable. Neither of us seems to know where to put our hands, because when they go on the table it seems like we're two criminals trying to show we have no guns and when we put them on our knees it seems like we actually do. Any second one of them is going to go off. He talks about the weather and I mention the book I'm reading, but underneath I can feel our fingers on their respective triggers. All it would take is for him to make a tiny move to the right.

Or for me to make a massive move to the left.

Like the move I actually make, in the middle of him saying how brave I was during the fire. "Those girls might have died if it weren't for you," he says, and then it just kind of happens. The tension of holding my finger on the trigger proves too much. The heat boils up to some impossible point and forces me to bridge the gap, far harder than I intend. I think I just want to hold his hand.

It seems like he wants to hold mine.

And hand-holding is much less than a kiss so it should be okay.

But what I end up doing is definitely not that. I somehow find the inside of his thigh—though I only know I have when he reacts. He immediately stiffens, and tries to look at me without looking, and stops talking so abruptly someone might as well have sliced his tongue in half. When I glance at him his lips are still parted around whatever word he was going to say.

Though at no point does he try to move my hand away.

He just glances in the direction of the page turner, hidden somewhere beyond the shelves that shelter us. As though to double-check that we are not going to be caught, I think, then get this sweet throb all the way through my body. He might actually let me, if the only thing that really worries him is whether anyone can see. He could accept more than a hand on the inside of his thigh.

Which is probably why I try. I lean toward him, eager to feel more of his heat and his body, so sure that this is it I kind of lose my mind a little. I rub my front against his arm when I only mean to rest there, and I know I'm breathing too hard and too hot. It almost sounds like I'm moaning. He looks at me like I am, at any rate. After a second of my shameless behavior he turns back real slow and stares at me.

As though he can hardly believe I'm this person.

He has to ask, just to make sure.

"Are you really this excited?" he asks, in a voice so full of incredulity it comes out hoarse. It makes me flush all over, and want more than anything to say no. *No it was just a temporary madness*, I imagine myself saying, but what would be the point? I know my body will make a liar out of me. Even now I'm still squirming. When I press hard against my chair it feels so warm and sweet I don't really want to stop—not even if he carries on raising that one terrible eyebrow at me.

Not even if his eyes keep gleaming like that.

Not even after he takes ahold of my hand, and puts it back in my own lap. "You know that I can't," he says, "you

know I can't let you do that, no matter how much you
might want to." And I do know. I know so much that I
go to stand, rather than spend another second under this
pressure, with this temptation bearing down on me like
he is the one suggesting that we eat the apple and I am the
one supposed to resist.

Though it gets harder to be sure who is who, when he
stops me with these words:

"But I can do this, if you like."

Such a simple way to put it, really. The *do* could refer
to anything. The *if you like* sounds close to the way people
talk about small favors. Only this is not small and it is
not a favor. I don't even think it would be if I was his
girlfriend and he was my boyfriend, though that might
be down to how stunning it feels. I never heard no one
talk about it being this stunning. Caitlin told me it was
nothing, but Caitlin was wrong.

When he puts his hand over mine and presses it
between my legs, I sorta want to sob.

"I can make *you* feel good. You *should* feel good," he
says.

And then I want to sob some more. I want to tell
him: *good* is not the right word. But if I do I will have
to explain, and I'm not sure there *are* words to describe
this sensation. It feels like my whole body has made a
fist, after years of being forced to lie flat. All this warmth
gushes through me, and of course it pools in the place he
is touching.

Oh Lord, he is touching me *there*. On that word Caitlin used.

"Pussy," she said, "don't you say pussy?"

And I could hardly tell her that I never use no words at all. I just say *there* and *between* and *my parts*, as though my pussy is some separate place to the rest of me. But I can't really do that anymore. It isn't a separate place now. It seems so suddenly hot and swollen that I got to admit it exists. That it does things, when he cups it with one big hand over my hand, and squeezes just a little.

If I don't, Lord only knows what will happen when he does more.

Because oh my God I think he might do more. He's looking at me in this searching way, eyes greedy for every one of my reactions. Just waiting for the right one to be there, before he goes on. And I know for a fact that he's going to find it. Not sure you could mistake someone arching their back and opening their mouth in a big shocked O.

And you definitely couldn't mistake a million whispered *pleases*.

Yet still, it kind of stuns me when he goes ahead. Or maybe it's *how* he goes ahead. I expect him to just rub oh I would die for just rubbing, I would writhe and moan for just rubbing I know I would, but he goes one better than that. Ten better than that, in fact, because the truth is we are still in a library and he is still three weeks away from being a Priest and neither of those things sits well with pushing up a girl's skirt.

Plus there is the *way* he does it.

He yanks and shoves and looks at me all the way through it, in a way that says *yeah sure this is absolutely all about you getting something sweet but maybe just maybe there's something in it for me, too.* Something frantic and feverish. Something that makes him lean over me too much and breathe too hard and put that skirt all the way up to the tops of my thighs—even though technically he doesn't need to. He could just lift it to my knees and get the same effect.

But he goes further.

He wants to see, I think blindly, wildly, and that idea is more exciting than all the rest of this combined.

Or it is until he touches me, without an extra layer of material or my own hand in the way. Just through my panties this time, and oh my word the difference is appalling. His fingertips are fire on me. Every point of contact burns, and then seems to swell. By the time he pulls away—just long enough to ask if this is what I need—the whole of my sex feels full and heavy, like some overripe fruit.

I practically drag him back, almost sure I must have been mistaken about exactly how it felt. It seems like too much. It seems like no one should have to bear something this intense. But when he does it again it somehow gets *worse.* He runs two fingers right over the seam that runs down the middle of me, pushing hard enough against the cotton to part things just a little bit.

And I have to grab his hand for a different reason.

Not to make him do it again.

To make him stop for a second *oh please stop* I don't know how to deal with this. My body is only just used to tiny pleasures—the taste of extra cinnamon in an apple pie that I didn't have to make, the comfort of a bed with a real mattress, the feel of clothes that aren't threadbare. It isn't prepared for this great big glut of it, to the point where it starts doing weird things.

My teeth keep clacking together, the way they might if I was randomly getting electric shocks. Every part of me is perspiring madly. And though I try to contain it, I'm shaking and shuddering all over. I do it so much that he leans back, and the stroking slows. "Calm down," he says, but how can I when he keeps doing that? He's making circles now, and boy oh boy are they sweet.

But somehow he don't know that.

"I can stop anytime you want I can stop," he says, as though my reaction is somehow panic or discomfort. And I can't even set him right, because when I open my mouth to do it, all that comes out is a thin, needy whine. Sounds like something dying, which of course makes his concern seem correct. He goes to move back the second I do it, and only my body stops him. My disobedient body, so stuffed full of pleasure that the evidence of it is right there for him to so easily find.

Though Lord, it makes my face heat when he does. I see it in the way he stiffens the moment he feels it, and want to put my hands over my eyes. I could just about cope with him watching me squirm and sigh, but this is something different. It seems so filthy somehow, so naughty of me—to not only do all of this with an almost Priest in a church library, but get so wet over it that when he goes to pull away he can feel it on the inside of my thigh.

Surely that must be crossing some line. *Surely*, I think, about a second before his eyes do that rolling hazy thing and his mouth finds mine. All in one rushed move, as though he couldn't wait for the asking or the explanations. He just has to do it, same way he has to put his hand right back to where it was. Only this time, he don't seem to worry so much about being careful. He pushes aside the material without a second thought or word, so obviously wanting to feel for sure that it does something weird to me.

It makes me moan into his mouth. It makes me rut up against his hand, head full of all the stuff he can feel. I'm so slippery that his fingers barely graze anything at all— they just glide over and through in a way that should be disappointing. But it isn't. It gets me even hotter. It makes me even wetter. I feel a slow wicked trickle of it between the cheeks of my backside and want to die.

Though if I did I would do it happy.

I have a love, and he is kissing me and touching me, and not saying a word about sin. He should be the one most concerned about it in all the world, and instead he does this. He gasps into my mouth over the evidence of my arousal, his kisses so open and heated I can hardly keep up with them. And the way he strokes me…not shyly or softly or unsure. He knows, I think, he really knows what to do to make me burst.

Heck, he knows better than I do. I got some notion about myself—some idea that I have a little bud like everyone else and that it feels good when I press the heel of my hand over it. But beyond that there is nothing but darkness and doubt, and places I'm not sure I can go.

So it seems like a miracle when he takes me there. He finds that thing—*my clit*, I think, *my clit*—with almost no effort at all, even though Caitlin said it takes men all the effort in the world. And then he just makes these little circles, these little nothing circles that should by all rights leave me bored. They should seem like nothing, I reckon, and instead they are everything ever. I almost shut my legs around his hand, they feel so good. I nearly bite my tongue in two.

I thought the hand over my panties was bad.

But this is something else. Reminds me of putting a freezing-cold hand into a bowl of hot water. White-hot lightning shoots up my spine, and suddenly I have no control over any of my limbs. My legs go out stiff and straight beneath the table and my hand clutches at his back. Tomorrow he'll have marks, I think blindly, but there ain't nothing I can do about that. I can only go with this.

This *bliss*, this utter and complete bliss. The hot swell of my clit and the ache and the ache of it as I spiral up and over into what is definitely an orgasm.

And most of all oh most of all:

The absolute and complete knowledge that I am finally free.

That this is what my freedom should truly be.

Chapter Ten

I REALIZE ON the third day that I probably got the wrong idea. I come away from his kisses in the library thinking that he might really want to be with me and I might really want to be with him, head stuffed full of all the thrilling things we can do together. I read in this one book about kissing him in places while he kisses you in places and I almost vibrate wondering on it. I dream about it at night and have imaginary conversations with him on the subject, so flush with all of this new knowledge that I hardly stop to think why he never comes.

Not to the library. Not to the hotel. I get no notes slipped under my door or secret phone calls, even though I know that's what people having affairs do. So I guess there's only one explanation: it was nothing it was just nothing. It was a moment of madness in the library.

Though I want to believe otherwise. So much so that one night I just can't stand staring up at my ceiling anymore, and do something real foolish. More foolish than any other thing I've done—but also more exciting and sort of fierce I guess. I feel like the wind is in me as I cross the courtyard to the dormitory he lives in. No part of me hesitates. I go right in and climb the stairs in the strange blue light of the approaching dawn, still in my nightdress but not caring in the least.

If they catch me I might even say:

I came to seduce one of the students.

Because I think I intend to do that, too. I can still taste that pleasure on my tongue. Part of me holds out some hope that it was not the only one I will ever get.

And then I see his expression when he opens the door, and I start to understand.

"You can't be here. You can't be in here," he says.

At which point I know for sure. I get it before he even adds more, and try to leave before he can. It won't be the end of the world after all. It's not like I love him and only him and can't live without him. *Not like the song,* I think. My heart will not be broken by something he never promised and could never give me and I should never ask for—or so I think until I babble at him that I understand.

"I understand that you have vows to take," I say, as I go to get away.

About a second before I feel his hand on my arm, pulling me back. And his expression—shaded by darkness but still so brutally clear. His eyes drink me in, as though those three days apart were a drought. Those dark brows remind me of thunderstorms, and when he speaks he don't even try to be quiet. We're surrounded by doors and through each one is probably a man who would denounce everything he then says.

But he does it anyway.

"I think you know I will never now take those vows. I think you know me enough to feel how little I want that life in every gesture and look and word," he tells me, so heartfelt I could never mistake it.

Yet I have to ask all the same.

I have to have it explained.

"Then why do you stay away?"

"Oh, Dot. Is that what you think?"

"I don't know what else I *could* think. You keep on leaving me to my own devices—which makes sense really because what else are you supposed to do? Throw it all away over some raggedy girl with crooked teeth and fool ideas about—"

"Stop, just stop. I thought you knew. You have to know. You have to know it isn't the idea of vows that keeps me from you," he says, and for just a second I puzzle over it. I imagine other things, dark, weird things like he has no penis or is secretly in love with Father Lucas, before he spells it out. "You were in my *care*, Dot—I'm meant to look after you. I can't pretend for one moment that the things you feel are not influenced by me coming to save you," he says.

He even does it like that's a big deal, or something I never thought of once.

I think possibly because he's a bigger fool than I am. I can hardly breathe thinking of how big a fool he is. All these weeks and months we spent apart—the way he said we shouldn't see each other and made us pray instead of every other thing we could have been doing. Does he not realize we could have been doing them?

"Is that all? Is that the only reason you stayed away all these times? Not because you made a promise to God or anything like that?"

"You say that like it's nothing," he says, at which point I almost feel mad.

Something like anger is in my voice when I speak, at any rate.

"Because it *is* nothing. If you wanted more than anything else to dedicate your life to the Lord, I would stand aside in a heartbeat. I did stand aside, thinking that was the reason you kept yourself from me. But now I know for sure it isn't. You should hear this, Killian: I might seem like some naive country girl who is gooey-eyed over some hero, but I got full as much sense as you and the same kind of heart and if God had graced me with a better life than the one I had, I would have done things just as I did. Only difference being that I could have met you as an equal and saved myself the pain of hearing you say this."

"I don't want to cause you pain, Dot."

"Then see me as I am. As someone who has been given space to make my own choices and is making them. I choose you, Killian. And if you choose me then don't let nothing stand in the way. Let me save you from a life you don't want—one made for you by circumstance and not the true song of your own soul. I can do it, and God knows I will if you want me to."

I run out of breath halfway through my speech, and have to strain to get the rest out. But I do it. I push and push until there's no more of anything left me, all my feelings right out in the open for him to see. Every inch of me trembling for his answer, so sure it will be more of the same. There are so many ways he could point out my weakness. So many arguments for him taking some advantage of me that even I can see them. I am poor and lonely and abused and neglected.

Of course I fell in love with someone like him.

What other explanation could there possibly be?

Other than the one he then gives me. The one where he abruptly pulls me to him and his lips find mine and oh, oh. *That* is the thing I love: his sudden bursts of passion like some overflowing thing, pouring and pouring through all of me. The way he grips my upper arms and kisses as though nothing in the world could ever stop him and always, always does the opposite of whatever I expect.

I reckon it will finish there.

But boy am I ever wrong about that. The moment I kiss back he decides to damn near lift me off my feet. He hauls me up so fast and so firm I have to throw my arms around his neck just to keep myself steady, but of course that only makes everything more intense. Now I'm holding on to all of him and pressed to every inch of him. It would take almost nothing to put my legs about his body, too.

So I do.

I do it just like they do in movies, without wondering for a second if I should. Why would I need to, when shoulds are a thing of the past? Nothing is forbidden, in this new place we've stumbled into. I've said the magical words or he's said the magical words and now this is where we are: tangling together so tight I doubt a crowbar could pry us loose. Barely sensible of our surroundings because our surroundings are something that isn't each other.

And all that matters is that. All I can feel is his mouth, working and working over mine. All I can taste is him, courtesy of the flickering licks he makes over my lips and the ones I get to do back. I get to just about f-u-c-k his mouth with my tongue and he don't care nothing about it. I reckon he likes it. No—I know he *loves* it, because he only goes and moans for me right there in the hall where anyone can hear.

Then again, for the hand I put on his face.

Mainly because I think he knows why I do it. I want to hold him there so I can do it harder. So I can do it more. I want to climb under his skin and settle there forever, and every single thing I do makes that real clear. My right leg is just about squeezing him to death, and I get where my left hand has gone. It still makes me flush to think on it, but I won't deny it.

I'm clawing halfway down his back.

And I ain't doing it on the outside of his T-shirt. I got my fingers past his collar somehow and so here we are. Me groping his bare back and him loving it enough to do one gut-punching thing the moment he gets me into his dorm and onto his bed. He don't even close the door first. He just takes a tiny step back—so tiny it barely counts, so tiny I only *almost* die of wanting—and hikes that T-shirt up over his head. All the way off just like that, just like it might be nothing.

Even though it's everything.

He hardly looks like I thought he would underneath his clothes. I thought he would be smooth all over the way his face is and just as milk-pale, but he isn't even remotely. His chest is covered in hair as black as the stuff on his head, so thick and rough my insides do this odd little hiccup. I see how it makes a line to the waistband of his pajama bottoms and the way it sprawls up to his shoulders, and some jerking thing just happens.

And then again when I take in how *big* he is.

Was he this big before? I mean I knew he was tall, but those shoulders didn't seem to be there when he was in his clothes. They look like marble tops of fancy pillars, all hard and round and too enormous. Every bit of him is hard and round and too enormous. He has muscles, real muscles like the men in magazines, and they all shift and stretch when he leans down toward me.

Really it's no wonder my hands go to him before he speaks.

Though I'm glad he does it anyway.

"Go on, go on do it everywhere, do it all over," he says, and I get immediately what he means. This is why he ripped off the shirt; this is why he brought me in here. Because he wants more of my hands on his bare skin. The hand I groped over his back was not enough, not nearly enough, and Lord that thought is a fire on my soul. It takes what would have been a tentative touch all the way up to this greedy uncontrollable grasping. I squeeze his shoulders and his biceps and all the parts in between, shove my fingers through that fur in rough strokes, find things I barely knew existed, and revel in each one.

He has jutting hip bones, like a girl, like my own.

Dimples above the curve of his backside that I can dip my finger into and stripes of muscle that point down to his groin. And all of it, all of it oh all of it feels good. It gets me shivering and shaking before we've really done anything, nipples already spiky and that thick heat between my legs. *I'm wet*, I think, *I'm wet*, and I get no mortification over the thought. I want to be that way, because I think he might do something.

Something more than just kissing and touching.

And I'm right, too. He *does* do more.

He does *everything*. Most of it all at once, like a ravenous animal suddenly let loose at a banquet after years of eating bread and water. One hand tries to push my nightdress up and the other runs all over my bare body, kissing and kissing and kissing me as he goes. And when I say kissing I don't just mean on the mouth, I mean over every part of me he can find, just like he said in that motel room. Every part he uncovers, from the curve of my belly to the insides of my arms to other places, naughtier places, places I might blush over.

If I wasn't doing the exact same thing right back at him.

I don't just lie there waiting for him to relieve this ache. I let the ache guide me. It gets sweeter and finer when I mouth a hot wet path over his collarbone, then heavier as I twist and try to get lower. Sounds crazy but I want to *bite* one of his nipples—just to see if it does the same things mine do. And I would have done it too, I would have gotten to it.

Only he gets there first.

I feel him turn and then there it is.

His mouth on me. His tongue flicking at rubbing over the stiff little tip of my one bared breast, back and forth and around and around until I think I might go out of my mind. How does he know what to do when it comes to these filthy things? He must have had girlfriends before, I think, but if he did I kind of doubt it would all feel exactly the way it does. Like he's operating on some of the same instincts I am, just blindly going for whatever feels best. Devouring me, the way I want to devour him. Pulling off clothes, the way I want to pull off his. Something of his rips when I tug too hard, and we both end up very tangled in my nightdress.

Very tangled, but very naked, too.

Oh Lord, he is *so* naked. There is so much of him suddenly that I hardly know what to touch or taste first. It seems like I should start small, but how can I when I can see just about everything now and all of it is brushing me and pressing into me? I got his gorgeous-looking thigh between mine and that was definitely a glimpse of his butt. I might be half-drunk on kisses and so greedy I keep forgetting to breathe, but I know that much. And I know another thing, too.

I know what that is lying heavy and solid against the inside of my thigh. I barely dare look or ask or feel it out with my hands, but I know. My reaction to it tells me enough—I moan his name at the idea of it. I grow hot and restless in a way I wasn't before, thinking and thinking on what might happen now. That thick shape is already so close to the place I want it to go. He would hardly have to move at all.

And I can see he's thinking on it.

He goes real still suddenly, and just looks down at me. Eyes so soft with feeling for me I could lie right down in them, every curve and facet of his face too beautiful in the strange blue light of this little room. I have to put my hands on him there, and when I do his reaction tells me what I need to know. His eyes stutter closed and the rest of him tenses, like he's waiting he's just waiting for me to do the rest.

He wants me to persuade him.

He wants me to ask him.

And I do—I just don't do it with words. I do it with my hands, fumbling and far too eager but finding him just the same. Finding that hot heaviness against my thigh, so much harder than I imagined and so much bigger, too. I always thought people exaggerated but I guess with him that's not true. He feels enormous, impossible, like some great root of a tree too big to see the top of. I can only just get my fingers around it, and when I squeeze it hardly gives at all.

Though he reacts.

Oh yeah he reacts. His hand snaps down between our bodies and gets a hold of mine, as though that pressure I put on was more like an electric shock. It sizzles up his spine, making everything seize as it goes, and when it's done it forces a sound out of him. A good one too—breathless and guttural, like he's got some gravel in the back of his throat. Might even be a *no* in there somewhere, though if there is it ain't the usual kind. It seems to mean something else, because that hand stays over mine.

It don't push me away.

There's no moving, but there's no pushing away.

And after a moment of staring and almost kissing and too much tension, I can see why. It feels too good to let it go. He wants to do other things, thoughtful things, unhurried things that ease me into this, but easing someone in is only possible when the hand around your cock don't make you shake. 'Cause I swear, that's what I think he might be doing. He's shaking because I'm touching him like this, because I circled him there. More than that in fact. His breathing is short and fast and I can see the flush on him even in the dark.

Then there's the slipperiness I can feel.

It ain't from me. It's from *him*.

Everything is all glossy down there and dimly I know why.

What I don't expect though is to *like* it so much. Oh my God in heaven I like it. The way it slides around under my fingers and makes it easy to stroke—even when he tries to hold me still. Just knowing he's this riled, so riled he reacts like a woman to this, like me the way I am between my legs…

It all combines to get me hot and bothered and just about desperate to do more. I want to see him. Heck, I want to *taste* him. I just got to get closer, but when I try he seems beside himself about it. He asks me in a voice like something falling down if I'm really going to do that, and we both know what he means. He sees what I want to do. He sees me straining to take him in my mouth, and he pulls me up short.

I just thank the Lord he does it in such an amazing way.

Here I am thinking he just wants to fight me on all the best things, the really rude things, and instead he goes and does the rudest of all. He gets a hold of me 'round my waist and heaves me up the bed, and while I'm still busy flailing and trying to touch him again he just goes for it.

"You have to go first," he says.

And then he licks me.

Between my legs.

Right over my pussy, even though I know my pussy is just about as wet as you please and so plump it could probably pass for a fist. But he don't care. I think caring disappeared some time ago and now there's just this: his mouth all soft and squirmy on my most sensitive parts, dipping and pressing and licking until I kind of want to punch something.

And right when I think I can't take anymore, I remember what he said.

You first, he said. As though he's gonna be second.

When this is done he might let me, and oh man that isn't going to be long. The idea of it alone is enough to push me higher. I think on it—of his cock slowly sliding back and forth past my lips—and I get that burst of sensation spreading outward from my stiff little bud. The bud that he then laps at softly oh so softly, building it and building it until I feel sure I can't take anymore. Surely this is the limit to the amount of pleasure someone can have in them. Every inch of me is tingling and aching. I feel like I need to clench hard down on something.

But that's okay.

He provides it.

He strokes me with two of his fingers and at first I think that's all it's gonna be. Just those two maddening fingers rubbing over all my curves and slopes and whorls, sliding so deliciously through everything without ever really going anywhere. But then I feel him there. Right over where I go in. I feel him working over it in this real specific way and right when I think he won't he does. He just glides all the way in, easy as you like.

No pain, the way they say there'll be.

No sudden lightning bolt from God striking me dead.

Though I suppose there should be. I'm on the bed of a seminary student's with his tongue on my clit and his fingers in my pussy and in a second, he's going to let me suck his cock. Nothing could be more wicked, I think, and nothing could feel less like it is. Instead it seems divine to me, as sweet as the sky on a summer day and twice as open. Twice as bright. No sunlight compares with the pleasure pouring through me. He gives one last twist of his fingers and one last lick, and that's when it hits.

The sudden rush. The heated waves.

My orgasm, I think, without shame.

I even call out his name. "Killian," I say, and I must do it in an exciting sort of way. Because the moment it bursts out if me, he responds in kind. He moans into my swollen and slippery sex, drawing my pleasure out like nothing else. I almost die at the hands of it. I shudder so much my teeth come close to catching my tongue. And I nearly forget, in the aftermath, what I wanted to do.

That this was supposed to be about him, too. He said I should go first which means by rights he should go second, only while I lie there dazed he decides to take it upon himself to steal that from me. He must have guessed, I think, how I would be after the fact. He hit me with that on purpose, so he could try putting on his clothes again once it was over with.

But he has to know I ain't never gonna let him do that. The second I see him trying to sneak his way back into his pajama bottoms—as though he is the shamed woman in all of this and I am the guy sitting pretty—I sit up. I do more than sit up, in fact. I reach out a hand and grab hold of his waistband, and I yank on it.

Much to his astonishment.

"What are you doing?" he blurts out, as though everything we just did was a dream and now that he is awake he gets to avoid it all. Like me, after those dreams I had about him.

Only with his actual mouth prints still all over me and a river running between my legs because of a real thing he did. He licked my clit, and now he wants to stop. He even tells me that directly: "We have to stop there."

Though he makes a mistake in the middle of it.

"You say *we*, but that don't seem right to me. I think you mean that *you* want to stop there. Whereas I think it's only fair that we go on."

"This isn't a matter of fairness, Dot. We're not playing checkers."

"No, if it were checkers it would be called outright cheating, me getting all the pieces while you get none at all."

"That is…a weird way to look it."

"A true way though, right? Twice now you made me feel so good I could cry over it. I never knew anything could be so sweet like that, but you want to deny me the chance to give you the same? Over what? Over vows you told me you don't care about?"

"You know it's not the vows."

"Then it's my maidenly virtue."

"I hadn't even got to your maidenly virtue in my head. Mostly when I think about this—" he starts, but then seems to reconsider before he finishes. He goes quiet after that word, and it's obvious even to me why that might be.

Obvious, and sort of a revelation.

"You think about this?" I ask after a second, in a voice that sounds way too curious.

So much so that he has to take a breath before he answers me. I even think for a second that he might not, which makes the things he does say all the more electric.

"Of course I do. All the time. Constantly. Every second of every day. Do you ever doubt that? If you do then let me be blunt—I imagine doing all of this to you and when I do, I masturbate. I spent most of the time in my

hotel room masturbating, just so I could carry on func-
tioning like a decent, reasonable person."

He said *masturbating*. He had to *function*.

I mean, on some level I knew these things. And I
know them better now. But to hear them out loud and
put like that is something else altogether. It sends a pulse
of heat through my body, despite all the stuff he just did.
It makes me look back over every little thing he did, and
see it suddenly set on the edge of some terrible precipice.
Him always about to go over, always about to do something wicked, and only ever stopping by taking that thick
length in his hand and stroking and sliding and oh, oh.

Is it any wonder my voice sounds faint, when I finally
speak?

"So all that time I was having dreams about you—"

"I had more than dreams about you, too."

I like how he says *more than*. Dreams are your mind
spewing up stuff against your will, but if you do it when
your eyes are open then you must really mean it. He
really meant it all the way back then, and just never said.

"Why didn't you tell me that?"

"I hate telling you *now*. I hated telling *myself*. Do you
have any idea how horrible it is to have this sweet young
girl in your charge and find yourself doing *that* because
of an accidental breast touch or the sound of some moaning that you pretend is distress when really you know it's
not?" he asks, and I almost gasp.

Only on the inside.

Way down deep on the inside, where everything is
slowly starting to boil over again.

"You did know then."

"I think I knew. I wish I hadn't."

"Why? Why? I *love* that you did," I say, even though *love* is too small a word. *Love* barely covers what all of this talk is doing to me. I seem to be rocking my hips like he's still there between my legs, and the hand on my thigh is not busy doing innocent things.

Despite how serious this conversation still is.

"Your love doesn't make me feel like less of a pervert."

"I'm twenty years old, Killian. I know my own mind."

"I know. I know. I know and yet—" he starts, then comes to an abrupt halt.

I don't blame him, though. I would probably come to an abrupt halt if he were doing the same thing I am. That busy hand on my thigh is now really not innocent at all.

And he has noticed. Even though my mostly discarded nightdress is partially concealing it, and everything is so dark in here, so dark…he has noticed. You can tell by that slight drop in his face—it always happens when I catch him off guard in some way. Every muscle seems to loosen just a little, and when he speaks it shows in his voice, too.

Oh I love how it shows in his voice.

That hint of hoarseness, as knowledge rubs up against disbelief.

"What are you doing?" he asks, and it's a pleasure to tell him straight.

"Touching myself. Thinking about you doing the same. Thinking about you in the hotel room next to mine with your hand on that big thing of yours."

'Course, I want to go with something other than *thing*.

I want to say *cock*—but am proud of myself all the same. It still makes his eyelids go low over his eyes and his eyes still roll up just a little. Plus that hoarseness oh that hoarseness is now a burr at the back of his throat. He seems to want to swallow it down.

But can never quite manage.

"That…that excites you?"

"Yeah. Oh yeah. Tell me how you did it."

"You want me to tell you how I masturbate," he says, half-incredulous and half-something else that sort of makes me worse. *He sounds excited*, my mind whispers, and then I just slide two fingers down, down, down through all of that slickness, just as easy as you please. Like he did it, I think, then marvel over the fact that it feels almost the same. I can do this to myself, with very little a trouble at all.

My little clit still jumps at the contact.

My pussy still clenches, waiting for me to do more.

And I will, right after I suggest something else.

"Unless you want to show me how you did it," I say, then wait for him to tell me no. Shake his head and make some counteroffer; give me something sweet instead of sordid.

I think that might be why I almost come when he answers.

"Probably not the way I'm going to do it now," he tells me, and I know what he means before I even ask him for clarification. "Why will it be different here?" I ask, but I know.

"Because here I don't have to feel so bad about it. Here I can just…" he says.

And then he brings his hand up to his mouth, and licks over his palm with that same wicked tongue he used on me. The little point of it briefly slides between his fingers, and leaves everything wet, so wet. None of which would be all *that* arousing, if I didn't have an idea of what he's doing it for.

Same reason I want to lick mine, before I touch one of my nipples.

It just feels better when you do. The glide is so sweet over your skin, and clearly it is for him, too. Why else would he do it before he eases himself from under his pajamas? Why else would he moan so much, when he makes one slick-looking stroke over that solid curve?

Because he does. He makes this long, low sound that sets my body to tensing, every part of me suddenly alive to the fact that this is really happening. He is really rubbing himself in front of me, all nice and slow and easy. That is honestly his cock, all stiff and swollen and just as big as I suspected it was not so long ago.

Looks like my right forearm, I think.

And that might be what pushes me to react the way I do.

"Oh my Lord. Oh. Oh. That…yeah," I moan, but only because I don't know that there is hotter to come. I think this is the limit—just him standing there stroking himself off, me drinking my fill of him with my eyes and trying not to overload myself with too-eager touches. But I am so wrong about that. So wrong.

Now it seems he's all riled up.

And he's got other things to say.

"I can just fuck myself slowly, slowly, slowly," he tells me, and all my insides jump over that *fuck* before he can even get out the rest. I'm rolling my hips and rubbing myself faster over that one word, but he has a bunch more. "Instead of fisting myself under the sheets while trying to think of something else. Instead of fucking myself too fast at the thought of you just like this, with that hand between your legs thinking of me."

He has so many more that I sort of lose it altogether.

"Ohh why does that sound so good? Why do I like that?" I ask, but he has no answers for me. I doubt he has any better than I do, considering how far gone he already is. His whole body is shuddering, now, and his hand is getting fast on that stiff, slick curve. Any second now and he might do it, which probably accounts for what I say.

"Let me touch you. Let me take you in my mouth."

"Ahhhh, *God*, don't say it like that. Don't say anything else," he chokes out, and when he does that hand speeds up, those eyes of his now down to slits. The sound of it so slick and filthy I just have to disobey him.

"I want to taste you. I want you to spill all over my tongue."

"Oh man. Oh man. Just—" he says, but I don't wait to see what he just wants me to do. Instead I simply lean forward right when he least expects it, and part my lips around whatever the slide of his fingers misses. The glossy tip of it, so smooth and so much sweeter than

anyone ever says this is. All of it is so much sweeter than
anyone ever says.

I think of Momma talking about wicked seed.

I think of Caitlin saying it hurts.

Then I feel him jerk forward, that thick length swelling and jumping against my tongue, the sound he makes
like his voice in song. I feel him spill in my mouth, and
see just how sweet it can be. Mainly because the same
thing happens to me. I become a flood in the wake of his,
my body giving in to that unbelievable bliss. I bow back
on the bed with the taste of him still there—like river
water on your skin after a long swim.

And just when I think nothing could ever be more of
a blessing than this...

He leans right down over me, to claim my mouth in
a kiss.

Chapter Eleven

HE TELLS ME to be patient with him while he goes through the resignation process, but the trouble with patience is that one person can be exactly that and still have everything fall to pieces. All it takes is the other person having none at all to push the house of cards over.

I just don't expect him to be the one without.

I expect it to be me. Barely a day goes by and I feel jittery, wondering on letters and how long they take to send and obligations that take far too long to meet. But I keep to my promise and respect him for trying to keep to his and so almost faint dead away when *he* comes to *my* door.

And not at any kind of decent time, either.

At four in the morning, when the hotel we are all staying in is as silent as the grave and Sister Marlena is snoring in the room next door. 'Course, I told him I wanted him to do this. I expressed this desire in a thousand different ways. But he keeps his desire so close to his chest sometimes that I occasionally forget it's even there. I think it's all me.

Right up until he groans, "I couldn't wait."

Then falls on me like some helpless shipwreck survivor. He was cast adrift in his own life, and now finally he's found someone who can help him swim to shore. I got my arm around him and he's got his arm around me, and together we can make it. And if our destination is rocky, so be it.

There is a sweetness in being scared that I can't deny.

It's the very thing that makes me moan when he spreads me out on the bed—just like before only not the same at all. Now there is the memory of that first time in us, and the reckless desire to go further. He dares to spread my legs and put himself between them, and I go even further than that. I slip my hand inside his jeans and feel for him.

And he don't even stop me.

He lets me, this time. I get to squeeze and rub and explore, so engrossed for a second that I almost forget that it might have an effect on him. He makes a noise and I jerk like somebody slapped me, glancing up just in time to see the greatest thing ever.

The sight of him enjoying himself. I *made* him enjoy himself. I got his head to go back like that, and his eyes to close. The sound he lets out is because of me, and so is the hand he then puts over his own mouth. He has to put a hand over his mouth, because whatever I'm doing feels good enough that he can barely control it.

And that thought is delicious to me, so delicious.

Much more so than it has any right to be. It makes me want to moan, too, and only the thought of Sister Marlena coming to see what might be going on keeps it in. The very last thing I want is for her to hear. If she does, I might have to stop this. I would probably have to take my hand out of his jeans, and that will not do at all.

Not when he's moving the way he's moving—just a little at first but then enough to make it unmistakeable. His hips are rolling and jerking and after a while I can feel the push of him through my fingers, until finally I know for sure. He's rutting into the circle I made around him. He likes it enough that he's rutting like some beast in heat.

An idea that damn near lays me out. That ache— the one that usually stays between my legs—swamps my whole body, so hot and thick I can hardly stand it. I feel like someone put a heavy hand on me all over, only a hundred times more awesome than that sounds. The hand presses on every good part there is: my already stiff nipples and my swollen bud and the clenching entrance to my pussy.

And when it does all of those things let off sparks. They send shivers down my spine and get me running like a river between my legs—enough that he almost chokes when he pushes under my skirt and finds what he finds. I swear I must have ruined the panties I have on. For a second he just slides around in all the mess, and when he speaks he sounds disbelieving.

"Why do you get like this? What made you like this?" he asks, but I don't feel embarrassed about it. When I flush all over, I do it because his words thrill me. They throb through me. I shake just to hear that strain in his voice, full well knowing what it means. It turns him on to know I get like this, over nothing.

To him, me being ready and ripe is not a crime.

It's a spur, driving him on. It makes his eyelids go heavy and his gaze get that haze over the top, mouth suddenly greedy for mine. Those fingers working and working through my slickness, until I am the one losing control. He finds my clit and worries it back and forth back and forth and I just about arch right off the bed.

But not before I get those jeans of his down.

Not before I show him what I have. I got it in the drawer by my bed, hidden under my clothes just in case, and I get it out. Even though I was thinking I would never and never talk about it and didn't even know at the time why I deposited ten coins to obtain it, I hand it to him. Then I wait, for him to object.

But he doesn't. He doesn't even stop to ask me where I got it or how. He just takes it from me and rips it open, and after that I know. There is nothing now that isn't allowed. This was the final line to cross—there are none beyond it. If he's willing to do this, then he means it. He means to be with me, I can see it. I can tell it before he even says, as he teeters on the brink of just sinking right in. I can feel him stroking me there over and over, his whole body shaking with the very idea, and then he says.

"I love you, Dot," he says.

And I love him back. I take him into me, without him asking or waiting on the right moment. I just ease him there slow slow slow, expecting pain and getting none.

Imagining him stopping me but never getting it. Instead, he laces his fingers with mine as he fills me, that wondering, disbelieving expression all over his face and all the better for it.

I love that he can hardly accept it. It thrills me to know that this was not what he thought it would be, either. Maybe somewhere inside him he had decided it was a sin, but if so all of that is gone now. He tells me it is gone. He whispers in my ear as he rocks, about how he never knew and never realized.

"I just didn't see that this was what I always wanted," he says. "I just didn't understand that all I needed was to love and be loved in return."

And I believe him. He makes it so easy to. The pleasure makes it so easy to.

How am I supposed to know that he's lying?

IT ALL SEEMS so simple and settled that I forget that life is rarely that way. I had even forgotten that there were obstacles still waiting for us to climb over.

So I guess that's why it's a more effective side-blinding when Father Lucas calls me into his office. I think we are already in the clear. I think all the barriers are removed and everything is finally open to me, that I am free and good and okay, and then I sit down in that creaking mahogany chair on the other side of his creaking mahogany desk and watch as the world I'd carefully constructed in my head falls apart.

"We can live in my father's old home," Killian had said. "I still have it."

But I guess they were just fairy tales, designed for a foolish girl.

Or at least they seem so, when I look into Father Lucas's eyes. They still have that way of seeing and not seeing you all at the same time. They make you seem as weightless as air, as meaningless as a word spoken in an empty room. And when he speaks, in that measured-but-brittle-around-the-edges voice of his, he does it so calmly and distractedly that you could nearly believe he was discussing something else.

"I think your time here at Saint Agatha's has come to an end," he says, and it just seems so mild. I almost miss the next part. I almost nod and say *oh yes I'm going to be making my own way soon*, but that just makes the one word he uses so shocking.

"There is no real place for whores here, you understand," he says, and just as my mind is wrapping itself around the fact that he said *whore, I think he said whore oh my Lord did he say whore* he carries on right the way into some swirling vortex of insanity. "I did so hope that Killian would be right about you and your mother wrong. But then he's such a susceptible boy, so vulnerable to the influences of Satan—that dreadful music he always listens to and so forth. I can't really fault him for giving in to your wiles. The devil assumes pleasing shapes, does it not?"

'Course I got no idea what to say to that. For a full thirty seconds I just stare at him openmouthed, so stunned that it sort of makes me pleased. I've come so far that I can barely believe anyone would speak like that.

None of this is normal to me anymore, and I make sure he knows it. I go to tell him why *I* know it.

"I'm not the devil. Sister Marlena—" I try to say.

But he just talks right over me.

Exactly like Momma used to.

"Oh, Sister Marlena is just as silly as your handsome young dupe. I did try to warn her about you, but she was just as taken in by your charms. The other girls, too. I had to take measures to show them your true nature, but alas it was seen as little more than an accident, a dreadful accident," he says, and then I start to explain to him again. I think of saying that I don't care what he thinks and Killian don't care what he thinks and none of this matters one bit, but before I can it dawns on me.

I see what he means, slow at first but then all in a rush.

"You…you set that fire."

"The demon inside you set that fire," he raps out, which seems insane considering he just told me he took measures. That means he did it, not me. That means he must be thinking irrationally about almost everything, but how am I to tell for sure? I can hardly catch my breath just to push aside the one main accusation—the thing I know is wrong but feels so right coming from someone as stern and cold and clever seeming as him.

"There is no demon in me."

"No? Then why did your mother think so?"

"Because my mother was mad."

"You're quite sure about that."

"Positive," I say, but inside I can feel the strain.

Suddenly I see very clearly what would have happened to me, if someone other than Killian had come along. Someone less *permissive*, I think, someone less susceptible, and want to draw myself into a tight ball of no this isn't right.

I need to, for the next part.

"Even though you fucked a boy four days away from his final vows. Four days away from his promise to God, four years of work thrown away so you could satisfy your filthy lusts and carnal desires."

I hate that he says *boy*. I hate that he says *promise to God* and *hard work* and uses the word *carnal*. Momma used to love that one so much, and applied it to almost everything I did. If I stayed in the bath too long, I was carnal. If I ate too much pie, I was carnal.

I don't even think she knew what *carnal* meant.

But I got this crawling suspicion that Father Lucas does.

He's an expert, after all. He might be going senile—in fact I think he definitely is, I know he is, somewhere inside me I'm certain I can see those two odd shoes behind my eyes—but being senile don't suddenly stop you knowing things. And maybe, just maybe he knows those things about me.

"None of those things make me a demon," I say.

But I can feel his knowledge creeping around inside me.

I can hear it coiling in his voice—so persuasive, he is.

Who would have thought those pale stones and that gray metal face and his barely there manner could be so persuasive?

"They sound like they do though, don't they?" he says, and I almost want to nod.

The only thing that stops me is remembering what Killian said.

"No. No. He made his own choices. He's not a boy. He's going to leave with me and—" I say, so sure of it suddenly that I almost see triumph.

He has no power over me, I think.

Only it seems I'm wrong about that.

"That's not what it says here," he says, so casual, so very casual and calm about it all that I feel forced to listen. If he was ranting and spitting and seemed all crazy on the outside I could just get up, I know I could. But instead he sits there as still and silent as a stopped clock, one finger ever so slightly touching a letter in front of him. A letter with Killian's handwriting all over it, I know. A letter that he claims—it must be only a claim, I think, please let it only be a claim—says something other than what we talked about.

"Here he tells me he deeply regrets his transgression," he says.

And then that falling I felt before starts to go much faster.

My face is as hot as a furnace when I respond.

There are tears in my eyes—tears that I hate almost as much as I hate him.

"You're lying. You're lying," I say, but I honestly have no clue if I still believe that.

He seems to be expanding and swelling in front of me. Soon I will hardly be able to avoid him.

"You filthy mouthpiece of whatever's crawling around inside you, you accuse me of lying? Well, I suppose if your mother was mad and your victim is in love it only stands to reason that I should be a deceiver. Or am I just sick, too? Am I unwell in my soul?"

Yes, I think, *yes you must be you set a fire you almost killed us.*

But the thing about it is: that voice in my head is so faint.

"I don't know. I don't know," I say, and for the first time I really don't.

He sounds so sure and sane. That voice of his makes even the devil and fire talk sound reasonable, and especially when he makes it into that soft little coil. He winds it around me, as easily as Killian twisted it away.

"You do know. Haven't you always suspected?"

Always, yes always every day of my life and more.

"Killian said that—" I start, but now he doesn't even have to interrupt me.

I stumble enough that he can just slip right in.

"Killian is a fool who thinks his father was mentally ill. I should never have let him go to you. I thought if he saw Satan as he really is he would understand but now I see I should have dealt with it myself," he says, just a little louder and a little fiercer than before, but a little is all it takes. He leans forward quite suddenly and I almost topple my chair I move back so fast. My face is wet and my heart is running a race in my chest, and over no more than a single finger that he points at me.

"Yes, go, leave here now," he says, and now I really am nodding. I imagine him getting up and grabbing me by the hair. I think of him tying me to a chair and I fumble my way toward the door. I don't even let him finish.

Though his voice carries enough that I hear him as I flee.

Perhaps if you never return, Killian can still be saved. And your soul, girl, your soul will be redeemed.

THERE IS A part of me that doesn't believe him. I think it might be the same one that climbed those stairs to Killian and told Caitlin that I thought God loved everyone and accepted that Momma was not quite right. I think it might understand that Father Lucas wasn't quite right, neither, and not just because of the things he said.

I recall Killian hesitating about him, too.

Maybe he knew, at the time, that something wasn't quite right. That Father Lucas was getting old or maybe even senile. Maybe, I think. But the trouble with *maybe* is how easily it bends beneath the weight of other factors. Other evidence and other ideas, all piling on top until finally that *maybe* breaks.

I break, after I speak to the man outside Killian's room.

Because of course I go there. Of course I do. I have to hear him say it with my own ears and see him do it with my own eyes—nothing less than that will satisfy, after everything we've been through together. All the promises and passion and love spilling over us both will not so easily be washed away.

By the time I get to his dorm room I feel almost easy about everything. It will be okay, I think. He will be in here waiting for me, and when I tell him that we should go now right now right with the bus tickets I got all by myself he won't shake his head or say otherwise. He will just get his things and come with me.

I feel sure he will.

And then I knock, and no one answers. He should be there, I know, because we were supposed to meet an hour from now anyway. He should be packing his things and making plans but all I hear on the other side of the door is silence. It makes me crazy, that kind of quiet. It ties my insides up into knots, to the point where I actually feel grateful when someone comes out of the room down the hall to talk to me.

"Are you okay there, miss?" he asks, and I am so relieved I answer him honestly. I say I'm looking for Killian, even though a girl should never be up here wondering about some student. Worse yet: I think I sound hopeful about it. Like I still think someone is going to tell me that everything will turn out okay.

But I guess life ain't really that way at all.

"I believe he went to pray," the guy says. "You know— for his sins."

And he does it so pointedly that there is no way at all I could mistake it for anything else. We both know what he means. He even underlines it for me with this look—this glassy look like the one Father Lucas gave me. He sees me without seeing me and shakes his head as though he knows.

Yeah, he could be lying all right. Both of them could be.

They could be in cahoots, most likely with the whole world.

Trouble is though, *could be* is not enough to fight off the rational reality of two separate people saying the same thing. And it sure isn't enough to fight off the other part of me. This one has spent too long in the dark, and remembers too well that time she pulled so hard on my wrist it broke, then made me stand there with it slowly killing me while she told Father Henry about the wicked thing I had done. It was only eating a candy out of the jar she kept—a fact that always told me just how wrong she was.

But now it works against me.

It sticks in my mind as I walk mindlessly back down the stairs and out the door, whispering to me about how small that single wicked deed was. And how big my wicked deeds are now, by comparison. If I get a broken wrist for stealing candy, what do I get for seducing a dupe, a boy, a poor confused seminarian on his way to the one true path?

My soul must be damn near snapped in two, I think.

Then keep right on walking.

I walk until my legs ache, hardly knowing where I'm going until I see the bus station up ahead. It comes right out of the dark at me, like some sign from God about what I should do. I got those tickets in my pocket after all…Just because he ain't gonna use his to get to the airport don't mean I can't use mine. Newark sounds as good a place as any to start over, seeing as how I got nothing to start over with. I have no money and no home and no nothing.

But none of those things really matter much to me, because I also have no Killian.

Even now, even though I should be sorry, I ache at the thought of having no him with me. I wonder and wonder what he wrote in that letter, until my head feels empty of anything but. Did he say it was all a mistake? Explain that I was to blame? I want to believe he never would, but he seemed to regret it once before.

The talk of demons and devils and fires might seem mad to me.

But the thought of his repentance does not. It seems so real I can almost hear him saying it—though I confess the voice in my head is only occasionally his. Most of the time it sounds like Momma or Father Lucas. Other times it sounds like me, trying to talk myself into this. After all, what did I possibly do to deserve someone as sweet as him? Nothing I did nothing and even if I had the whole thing was never right.

It is almost definitely better this way. I will go and he can carry on as he was before, moving on into his new life of goodness and purity and glassy-eyed looks at girls who might be whores. And I can move on into my new life— one that feels like the cold metal bench of a bus station, surrounded by angry people who stare too long.

Still, that seems better to me than what I had before.

I have a little money in my purse and can buy a sandwich.

When did I ever get to buy a sandwich before? Most days I survived on burnt potatoes and moldering bread, so this is still some kind of improvement.

The only problem is: I'm not sure how satisfied I am anymore with *an improvement*. I want to be God knows

I want to be. I wish my heart would stay in one piece and not start to crack under the pressure of this. I long to enjoy my little makeshift meal and be thankful for the bench to rest on. But the more I try the more I realize what his real gift to me was.

He made me hope for more than I could ever believe I might have. He gave that to me—that tiny ember burning bright in the most vulnerable part of my body. He made me see that people can be godly and good, that kindness is the highest virtue and love is something no one should shame away. And now those ideas are far too hard to shake. They make me think of him coming to save me even as the clock runs down to nothing. I imagine him pulling me out of the queue onto the bus, full of words about his mistake or their mistake, almost in despairing tears at the idea but somehow unable to stop. I doubt anything will ever make this whirligig of wishing and disappointment stop. It still happens once I'm sitting on the bus with nothing but darkness and strangers all about me, and the driver telling us two minutes to go.

I close my eyes and think: he will come.

At the last second, he will be here.

Even though I know that is just an idle fancy of the way things can be. In reality, no one really comes to save you. And if you're lucky enough to have it once, just once, just one time someone coming through the door to take you away from all of that madness, then surely it must be too much to wish for it again.

Surely it must be.

Surely it was all a sin.

And then I see him.

I see his face and think I must be dreaming, but if I am I never want to wake up. Just let me stay like this forever, with him suddenly there at the side of the bus. Those eyes of his so full of feeling for me in the exact same way I remember, yet so soon forgot. I forgot that he could fill me with love and relief and light with just one look. I allowed myself to erase his every heartfelt gesture—like the one he makes now.

He puts his hand against the glass.

He puts it there, and I know why. I see it all clearly in that one tiny thing, but then that has always been the way with him. This is how we grew to love each other, in the smallest of increments and the littlest of things. He said he loved me with a touch and asked me to be by his side with a glance, and the same thing happens here.

I never left you, that gesture says.

I will never leave you.

And I believe. I believe in him. I believe in me. So much so that I stumble off the bus and once outside I don't stop. There are no more moments of hesitation, me waiting for him to take that step across the distance between us. I just run to him, the way I always want to. He doesn't even have to say.

I know full well that I am saved.

That I am good, without the word of God. That I love, without the need for permission. That it is never a sin to do what we did, no matter who tells you otherwise.

Though Lord, I love hearing him explain anyway.

"Did you really think I would change my mind?" he says. "Did you really think an old and confused man who sets fires and is currently in the hands of dedicated health care professionals could convince me? That I would honestly write my regret in a letter and let him deliver those words to you?"

I love it even though it makes me a fool, and forces me to offer him a thousand sorries in one long tumble. I tell him about the boy in the hall who made it seem so real even though I can see now that he was just assuming or guessing or maybe even lying for the fun of it. I tell him about the sound of Momma in my head like a siren, voice hitching in all the wrong places and eyes just about begging him to understand.

I should really know by now though—he never does anything but. He takes my face in his two hands and says everything I never knew I always wanted to hear. "No one leaves behind their past. It will always be with you and always make you wonder and doubt, but when it does know this: I am here to make sure you never have to for long. I will always be here. I love you, Dot," he says.

And then I drift away on the sea with him.

My shipwreck survivor, almost with me at the shore. All our lives spread before us, now that the past is so far behind. I can barely see it from where we stand, and even less so after his kiss. Oh his kiss, so full of everything I felt over the past few hours, reflected back at me just the same. All that despair and sadness and uncertainty, burned down to nothing by his hand in my hair and his mouth on mine.

Every bit of it gone, and only this left behind:

I am his, and he is mine.

Epilogue

HE WAS LYING about the way Ireland is. None of it is gray and miserable at all. To me it looks like an ocean, if the ocean were made out of grass. I walk through endless waves every day, to our little cottage by the edge of the forest. And then we sit by the window and I tell him about the things I did in my library today, and he tells me about his students and the things they had to say, and when it gets dark and the sea of green stalks talk together in thick whispers he takes me up to bed.

He lays me down on our big brass bed, and the only thing that binds my wrists are his hands and the only thing that holds me there is his love. No thoughts of anything forbidden—now nothing is. I whisper in his ear every filthy thing I can think of that two people can do. I find books with new ways of doing this in them, and films with every wicked thing you can imagine.

And I pour them all into him.

I tell him, "Take me on all fours, like an animal." I say faster; I ask for harder. I give him everything I never knew I wanted and all the things I should hold back. There is nothing he will not allow me, and I love him for that.

But I love him more when he learns to do the same. Slowly, oh so slowly like a rock eroded down into flowing sand. He starts small, with simple things that barely seem like requests—just a hint here and there left for me to find. The way he rests his hand next to mine. The arch of his body as he strips for me, too deliberate to be anything but a tease.

Then finally the words, running deep from someplace near lost inside him.

That place he buried beneath his need to only give, to be good, to be better.

Now found in our love, in our bed, in our life together.

"Fuck me like you mean it," he tells me.

And I laugh.

I love.

I am.

About the Author

CHARLOTTE STEIN is the acclaimed author of over thirty short stories, novellas, and novels, including the recently DABWAHA-nominated *Run to You*. When not writing deeply emotional and intensely sexy books, she can be found eating jelly turtles, watching terrible sitcoms, and occasionally lusting after hunks. For more on Charlotte, visit www.charlottestein.net.

Discover great authors, exclusive offers, and more at hc.com.

Give in to your impulses . . .
Read on for a sneak peek at seven brand-new
e-book original tales of romance
from Avon Impulse.
Available now wherever e-books are sold.

HOLDING HOLLY
A Love and Football Novella
By Julie Brannagh

IT'S A WONDERFUL FIREMAN
A Bachelor Firemen Novella
By Jennifer Bernard

ONCE UPON A HIGHLAND CHRISTMAS
By Lecia Cornwall

RUNNING HOT
A Bad Boys Undercover Novella
By HelenKay Dimon

SINFUL REWARDS 1
A Billionaires and Bikers Novella
By Cynthia Sax

RETURN TO CLAN SINCLAIR
A Clan Sinclair Novella
By Karen Ranney

RETURN OF THE BAD GIRL
By Codi Gary

An Excerpt from

HOLDING HOLLY
A Love and Football Novella
by Julie Brannagh

Holly Reynolds has a secret. Make that two.
The first involves upholding her grandmother's
hobby of answering Dear Santa letters from
dozens of local schoolchildren. The second . . .
well, he just came strolling in the door.

Derrick has never met a woman he wanted to
bring home to meet his family, mostly because
he keeps picking the wrong ones—until he
runs into sweet, shy Holly Reynolds. Different
from anyone he's ever known, Derrick realizes
she might just be everything he needs.

"**D**o you need anything else right now?"

"I'm good," he said. "Then again, there's something I forgot."

"What do you need? Maybe I can help."

He moved closer to her, and she tipped her head back to look up at him. He reached out to cup one of her cheeks in his big hand. "I had a great time tonight. Thanks for having pizza with me."

"I had a nice time too. Th-thank you for inviting me," she stammered. There was so much more she'd like to say, but she was tongue-tied again. He was moving closer to her, and he reached out to put his drinking glass down on the counter.

"Maybe we could try this again when we're not in the middle of a snowstorm," he said. "I'd like a second date."

She started nodding like one of those bobbleheads, and forced herself to stop before he thought she was even more of a dork.

"Yes. I . . . Yes, I would too. I . . . that would be fun."

He took another half-step toward her. She did her best to pull in a breath.

"Normally, I would have kissed you good night at your front door, but getting us inside before we froze to death seemed like the best thing to do right then," he said.

"Oh, yes. Absolutely. I—"

He reached out, slid his arms around her waist, and pulled her close. "I don't want to disrespect your grandma's wishes," he softly said. "She said I needed to treat you like a lady."

Holly almost let out a groan. She loved Grandma, but they needed to have a little chat later. "Sorry," she whispered.

He grinned at her. "I promise I'll behave myself, unless you don't want me to." She couldn't help it; she laughed. "Plus," he continued, "she said you have to be up very early in the morning to go to work, so we'll have to say good night."

Maybe she didn't need sleep. One thing's for sure, she had no interest in stepping away from him right now. He surrounded her, and she wanted to stay in his arms. Her heart was beating double-time, the blood was effervescent in her veins, and she summoned the nerve to move a little closer to him as she let out a happy sigh.

He kissed her cheek, and laid his scratchier one against hers. A few seconds later, she slid her arms around his neck too. "Good night, sweet Holly. Thanks for saving me from the snowstorm."

She had to laugh a little. "I think you saved *me*."

"We'll figure out who saved who later," he said. She felt his deep voice vibrating through her. She wished he'd kiss her again. Maybe she should kiss *him*.

He must have read her mind. He took her face in both of his hands. "Don't tell your grandma," he whispered. His breath was warm on her cheek.

"Tell her what?"

"I'm going to kiss you."

Her head was bobbing around as she frantically nodded yes. She probably looked ridiculous, but he didn't seem to care. Her eyelids fluttered closed as his mouth touched hers, sweet and soft. It wasn't a long kiss, but she knew she'd never forget it. She felt the zing at his tender touch from the top of her head to her toes.

"A little more?" he asked.

"Oh, yes."

His arms wrapped around her again, and he slowly traced her lips with his tongue. It slid into her mouth. He tasted like the peppermints Noel Pizza kept in a jar on the front counter. They explored each other for a while as quietly as possible, but maybe not quietly enough.

"Holly, honey," her grandma called out from the family room. Holly was *absolutely* going to have a conversation with Grandma when Derrick was out of earshot, and she stifled a groan. All they were doing was a little kissing. He rested one big hand on her butt, which she enjoyed. "Would you please bring me some salad?"

Derrick let out a snort. "I'll get it for you, Miss Ruth," he said loudly enough for her grandma to hear.

"She's onto us," Holly said softly.

"Damn right." He grinned at her. "I'll see you tomorrow morning." His voice dropped. "We're *definitely* kissing on the second date."

"I'll look forward to that." She tried to pull in a breath. Her head was spinning. She couldn't have stopped smiling if her life depended on it. "Are you sure you don't want to stay in my room instead? You need a good night's sleep. Don't you have to go to practice?"

"I'm sure your room is very comfortable, but I'll be fine out here. Sweet dreams," he said.

She felt him kiss the top of her head as he held her. She took a deep breath of his scent: clean skin, a whiff of expensive cologne, and freshly pressed clothes. "You, too," she whispered. She reached up to kiss his cheek. "Good night."

An Excerpt from

IT'S A WONDERFUL FIREMAN
A Bachelor Firemen Novella

by Jennifer Bernard

Hard-edged fireman Dean Mulligan has never
been a big fan of Christmas. Twinkly lights and
sparkly tinsel can't brighten the memories of too
many years spent in ramshackle foster homes.
When he's trapped in the burning wreckage of
a holiday store, a Christmas angel arrives to
open his eyes. But is it too late? This Christmas,
it'll take an angel, a determined woman in love,
and the entire Bachelor Firemen crew to make
him believe . . . it is indeed a wonderful life.

He'd fallen. Memory returned like water seeping into a basement. He'd been on the roof, and then he'd fallen through, and now he was . . . here. His PASS device was sounding in a high-decibel shriek, and its strobe light flashed, giving him quick, garish glimpses of his surroundings.

Mulligan looked around cautiously. The collapse must have put out much of the fire, because he saw only a few remnants of flames flickering listlessly on the far end of the space. Every surface was blackened and charred except for one corner, in which he spotted blurry flashes of gold and red and green.

He squinted and blinked his stinging eyes, trying to get them to focus. Finally the glimpse of gold formed itself into a display of dangling ball-shaped ornaments. He gawked at them. What were those things made from? How had they managed to survive the fire? He sought out the red and squinted at it through his face mask. A Santa suit, that's what it was, with great, blackened holes in the sleeves. It was propped on a rocking chair, which looked quite scorched. Mulligan wondered if a mannequin or something had been wearing the suit. If so, it was long gone. Next to the chair stood half of a plastic Christmas tree. One side had melted into black goo, while the other side looked pretty good.

Where am I? He formed the words with his mouth, though no sound came out. And it came back to him. Under the Mistletoe. He'd been about to die inside a Christmas store. But he hadn't. So far.

He tried to sit up, but something was pinning him down. Taking careful inventory, he realized that he lay on his left side, his tank pressing uncomfortably against his back, his left arm immobilized beneath him. What was on top of him? He craned his neck, feeling his face mask press against his chest. A tree. A freaking Christmas tree. Fully decorated and only slightly charred. It was enormous, at least ten feet high, its trunk a good foot in diameter. At its tip, an angel in a gold pleated skirt dangled precariously, as if she wanted to leap to the floor but couldn't summon the nerve. Steel brackets hung from the tree's trunk; it must have been mounted somewhere, maybe on a balcony or something. A few twisted ironwork bars confirmed that theory.

How the hell had a Christmas tree survived the inferno in here? It was wood! Granted, it was still a live tree, and its trunk and needles held plenty of sap. And fires were always unpredictable. The one thing you could be sure of was that they'd surprise you. Maybe the balcony had been protected somehow.

He moved his body, trying to shift the tree, but it was extremely heavy and he was pinned so flat he had no leverage. He spotted his radio a few feet away. It must have been knocked out of his pouch. Underneath the horrible, insistent whine of his PASS device, he heard the murmuring chatter of communication on the radio. If he could get a finger on it, he could hit his emergency trigger and switch to Channel 6, the May Day channel. His left arm was useless, but he could try with his right. But when he moved it, pain ripped through his shoulder.

Hell. Well, he could at least shut off the freaking PASS device. If a rapid intervention team made it in here, he'd yell for them. But no way could he stand listening to that sound for the next whatever-amount-of-time it took. Gritting his teeth against the agony, he reached for the device at the front of his turnout, then hit the button. The strobe light stopped and sudden silence descended, though his ears still rang. While he was at it, he checked the gauge that indicated how much air he had left in his tank. Ten minutes. He must have been in here for some time, sucking up air, since it was a thirty-minute tank.

A croak issued from his throat. "I'm in hell. No surprise."

Water. He needed water.

"I can't give you any water," a bright female voice said. For some reason, he had the impression that the angel on the tip of the Christmas tree had spoken. So he answered her back.

"Of course you can't. Because I'm in hell. They don't exactly hand out water bottles in hell."

"Who said you're in hell?"

Even though he watched the angel's lips closely, he didn't see them move. So it must not be her speaking. Besides, the voice seemed to be coming from behind him. "I figured it out all by myself."

Amazingly, he had no more trouble with his throat. Maybe he wasn't really speaking aloud. Maybe he was having this bizarre conversation with his own imagination. That theory was confirmed when a girl's shapely calves stepped into his field of vision. She wore red silk stockings the exact color of holly berries. She wore nothing else on her feet, which had a very familiar shape.

Lizzie.

His gaze traveled upward, along the swell of her calves. The stockings stopped just above her knees, where they were fastened by a red velvet bow. "Christmas stockings," he murmured.

"I told you."

"All right. I was wrong. Maybe it's heaven after all. Come here." He wanted to hold her close. His heart wanted to burst with joy that she was here with him, that he wasn't alone. That he wasn't going to die without seeing Lizzie again.

"I can't. There's a tree on top of you," she said in a teasing voice. "Either that, or you're very happy to see me."

"Oh, you noticed that? You can move it, can't you? Either you're an angel and have magical powers, or you're real and you can push it off me."

She laughed. A real Lizzie laugh, starting as a giggle and swooping up the register until it became a whoop. "Do you really think an angel would dress like this?"

"Hmm, good point. What are you wearing besides those stockings? I can't even see. At least step closer so I can see."

"Fine." A blur of holly red, and then she perched on the pile of beams and concrete that blocked the east end of his world. In addition to the red stockings, she wore a red velvet teddy and a green peaked hat, which sat at an angle on her flowing dark hair. Talk about a "hot elf" look.

"Whoa. How'd you do that?"

"You did it."

"I did it?" How could he do it? He was incapacitated. Couldn't even move a finger. Well, maybe he could move a finger. He gave it a shot, wiggling the fingers on both hands. At least he wasn't paralyzed.

But he did seem to be mentally unstable. "I'm hallucinating, aren't I?"

"Bingo."

An Excerpt from

ONCE UPON A HIGHLAND CHRISTMAS

by Lecia Cornwall

Lady Alanna McNabb is bound by duty
to her family, who insist she must marry a
gentleman of wealth and title. When she meets
the man of her dreams, she knows it's much
too late, but her heart is no longer hers.

Laird Iain MacGillivray is on his way to propose
to another woman when he discovers Alanna
half-frozen in the snow and barely alive. She isn't
his to love, yet she's everything he's ever wanted.

As Christmas comes closer, the snow
thickens, and the magic grows stronger.
Alanna and Iain must choose between
desire and duty, love and obligation.

Alanna McNabb woke with a terrible headache. In fact, every inch of her body ached. She could smell peat smoke, and dampness, and hear wind. She remembered the storm and opened her eyes. She was in a small dark room, a hut, she realized, a shieling, perhaps, or was it one of the crofter's cottages at Glenlorne? Was she home, among the people who knew her, loved her? She looked around, trying to decide where exactly she was, whose home she was in. The roof beams above her head were blackened with age and soot, and a thick stoneware jug dangled from a nail hammered into the beam as a hook. But that offered no clues at all—it was the same in every Highland cott. She turned her head a little, knowing there would be a hearth, and—

A few feet from her, a man crouched by the fire.

A very big, very naked man.

She stared at his back, which was broad and smooth. She took note of well-muscled arms as he poked the fire. She followed the bumps of his spine down to a pair of dimples just above his round white buttocks.

Her throat dried. She tried to sit up, but pain shot through her body, and the room wavered before her eyes. Her leg was on fire, pure agony. She let out a soft cry.

He half turned at the sound and glanced over his shoulder, and she had a quick impression of a high cheekbone lit by the firelight, and a gleaming eye that instantly widened with surprise. He dropped the poker and fell on his backside with a grunt.

"You're awake!" he cried. She stared at him sprawled on the hearthstones, and he gasped again and cupped his hands over his— She shut her eyes tight, as he grabbed the nearest thing at hand to cover himself—a corner of the plaid— but she yanked it back, holding tight. He instantly let go and reached for the closest garment dangling from the line above him, which turned out to be her red cloak. He wrapped it awkwardly around his waist, trying to rise to his feet at the same time. He stood above her in his makeshift kilt, holding it in place with a white knuckled grip, his face almost as red as the wool. She kept her eyes on his face and pulled her own blanket tight around her throat.

"I see you're awake," he said, staring at her, his voice an octave lower now. "How do you feel?"

How *did* she feel? She assessed her injuries, tried to remember the details of how she came to be here, wherever here might be. She recalled being lost in a storm, and falling. There'd been blood on her glove. She frowned. After that she didn't remember anything at all.

She shifted carefully, and the room dissolved. She saw stars, and black spots, and excruciating pain streaked through her body, radiating from her knee. She gasped, panted, stiffened against it.

"Don't move," he said, holding out a hand, fingers splayed, though he didn't touch her. He grinned, a sudden flash of white teeth, the firelight bright in his eyes. "I found you out in the snow. I feared . . . well, it doesn't matter now. Your knee is injured, cut, and probably sprained, but it isn't broken," he said in a rush. He grinned again, as if that was all very good news, and dropped to one knee beside her. "You've got some color back."

He reached out and touched her cheek with the back of his hand, a gentle enough caress, but she flinched away and gasped at the pain that caused. He dropped his hand at once, looked apologetic. "I mean no harm, lass—I was just checking that you're warm, but not too warm. Or too cold . . ." He was babbling, and he broke off, gave her a wan smile, and stood up again, holding onto her cloak, taking a step back away from her. Was he blushing, or was it the light of the fire on his skin? She tried not to stare at the breadth of his naked chest, or the naked legs that showed beneath the trailing edge of the cloak.

She gingerly reached down under the covers and found her knee was bound up in a bandage of some sort. He turned away, flushing again, and she realized the plaid had slipped down. She was as naked as he was. She gasped, drew the blanket tight to her chin, and stared at him. She looked up and saw that her clothes were hanging on a line above the fireplace—all of them, even her shift.

"Where—?" she swallowed. Her voice was hoarse, her throat as raw as her knee. "Who are you?" she tried again. She felt hot blood fill her cheeks, and panic formed a tight knot in her chest, and she tried again to remember what had happened, but her mind was blank. If he was—unclothed, and she was equally unclothed—

"What—" she began again, then swallowed the question

she couldn't frame. She hardly knew what to ask first, Where, Who, or What? Her mind was moving slowly, her thoughts as thick and rusty as her tongue.

"You're safe, lass," he said, and she wondered if she was. She stared at him. She'd seen men working in the summer sun, their shirts off, their bodies tanned, their muscles straining, but she'd never thought anything of it. This—he—was different. And she was as naked as he was.

An Excerpt from

RUNNING HOT
A Bad Boys Undercover Novella
by HelenKay Dimon

Ward Bennett and Tasha Gregory aren't on the
same team. But while hunting a dictator on the
run, these two must decide whether they can trust
one another—and their ability to stay professional.
Working together might just make everyone safer,
but getting cozy . . . might just get them killed.

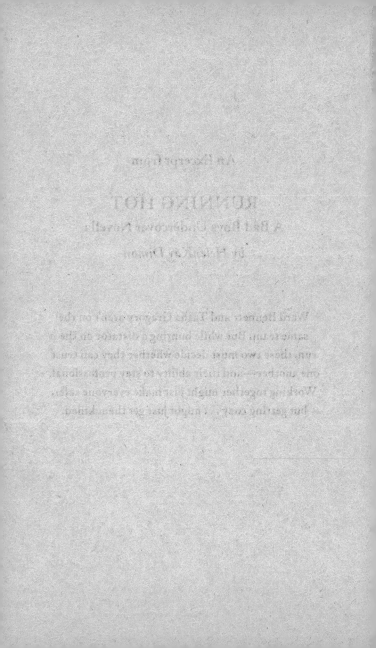

An Excerpt from

RUNNING HOT

A Bad Boys Undercover Novella

By HelenKay Dimon

"Take your clothes off."

He looked at her as if she'd lost her mind. "Excuse me?"

"You're attracted to me." Good Lord, now Tasha was waving her hands in the air. Once she realized it, she stopped. Curled her hands into balls at her sides. "I find you . . . fine."

Ward covered his mouth and produced a fake cough. She assumed it hid a smile. That was almost enough to make her rescind the offer.

"Really? That's all you can muster?" This time he did smile. "You think I'm fine?"

He was hot and tall and had a face that played in her head long after she closed her eyes each night. And that body. Long and lean, with the stalk of a predator. Ward was a man who protected and fought. She got the impression he wrestled demons that had to do with reconciling chivalry and decency with the work they performed.

The combination of all that made her wild with need. "Your clothes are still on."

"Are you saying you want to—"

Since he was saying the sentence so slowly—emphasizing, and halting after, each word—she finished it fast. "Shag."

Both eyebrows rose now. "Please tell me that's British for 'have sex.'"

"Yes."

He blew out a long, staggered breath. "Thank God, because right now my body is in a race to see what will explode first, my brain or my dick."

Uh? "Is that a compliment?"

"Believe it or not, yes." Two steps, and he was in front of her, his fingers playing with the small white button at the top of her slim tee. "So, are you talking about now or sometime in the future to celebrate ending Tigana?"

Both. "I need to work off this extra energy and get back in control." She was half-ready to rip off her clothes and throw him on the mattress.

Maybe he knew because he just stood there and stared at her, his gaze not leaving her face.

She stared back.

Just as he started to lower his head, a ripple moved through her. She shoved a hand against his shoulder. "Don't think that I always break protocol like this."

"I don't care if you do." He ripped his shirt out of his pants and whipped it over his head, revealing miles of tanned muscles and skin.

"You're taking off your clothes." Not the smartest thing she'd ever said, but it was out there and she couldn't snatch it back.

"You're the boss, remember?"

A shot of regret nearly knocked her over. Not at making the pass but at wanting him this much in the first place. Here and now, when her mind should be on the assignment, not on his chest.

She'd buried this part of herself for so long under a pile of work and professionalism that bringing it out now made her twitchy. "This isn't—"

His hands went to her arms, and he brushed those palms up and down, soothing her. "Do you want me?"

She couldn't lie. He had to feel it in the tremor shaking through her. "Yes."

"Then stop justifying not working this very second and enjoy. It won't make you less of a professional."

That was exactly what she needed to hear. "Okay."

His hands stopped at her elbows, and he dragged her in closer, until the heat of his body radiated against her. "You're a stunning woman, and we've been circling each other for days. Honestly, your ability to handle weapons only makes you hotter in my eyes."

The words spun through her. They felt so good. So right. "Not the way I would say it, but okay."

"You want me. I sure as hell want you. We need to lie low until it gets dark and we can hide our movements better." The corner of his mouth kicked up in a smile filled with promise. "And, for the record, there is nothing sexier than a woman who goes after what she wants."

He meant it. She knew it with every cell inside her.

Screw being safe.

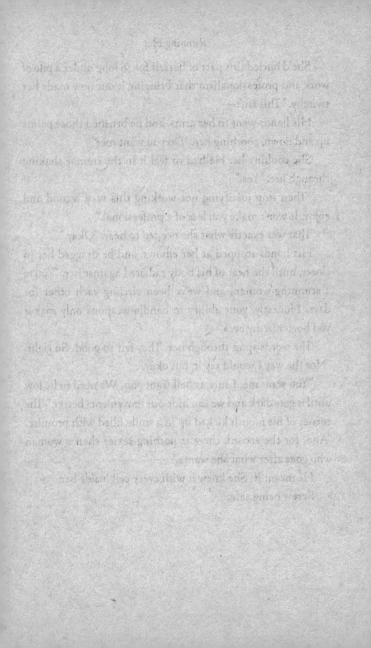

An Excerpt from

SINFUL REWARDS 1
A Billionaires and Bikers Novella
by Cynthia Sax

Belinda "Bee" Carter is a good girl; at least, that's
what she tells herself. And a good girl deserves
a nice guy—just like the gorgeous and moody
billionaire Nicolas Rainer. Or so she thinks,
until she takes a look through her telescope
and sees a naked, tattooed man on the balcony
across the courtyard. He has been watching
her, and that makes him all the more enticing.
But when a mysterious and anonymous text
message dares her to do something bad, she
must decide if she is really the good girl she has
always claimed to be, or if she's willing to risk
everything for her secret fantasy of being watched.

An Avon Red Novella

I'd told Cyndi I'd never use it, that it was an instrument purchased by perverts to spy on their neighbors. She'd laughed and called me a prude, not knowing that I was one of those perverts, that I secretly yearned to watch and be watched, to care and be cared for.

If I'm cautious, and I'm always cautious, she'll never realize I used her telescope this morning. I swing the tube toward the bench and adjust the knob, bringing the mysterious object into focus.

It's a phone. Nicolas's phone. I bounce on the balls of my feet. This is a sign, another declaration from fate that we belong together. I'll return Nicolas's much-needed device to him. As a thank you, he'll invite me to dinner. We'll talk. He'll realize how perfect I am for him, fall in love with me, marry me.

Cyndi will find a fiancé also—everyone loves her—and we'll have a double wedding, as sisters of the heart often do. It'll be the first wedding my family has had in generations.

Everyone will watch us as we walk down the aisle. I'll wear a strapless white Vera Wang mermaid gown with organza and lace details, crystal and pearl embroidery accents, the bodice fitted, and the skirt hemmed for my shorter height. My hair will be swept up. My shoes—

Voices murmur outside the condo's door, the sound piercing my delightful daydream. I swing the telescope upward, not wanting to be caught using it. The snippets of conversation drift away.

I don't relax. If the telescope isn't positioned in the same way as it was last night, Cyndi will realize I've been using it. She'll tease me about being a fellow pervert, sharing the story, embellished for dramatic effect, with her stern, serious dad— or, worse, with Angel, that snobby friend of hers.

I'll die. It'll be worse than being the butt of jokes in high school because that ridicule was about my clothes and this will center on the part of my soul I've always kept hidden. It'll also be the truth, and I won't be able to deny it. I am a pervert.

I have to return the telescope to its original position. This is the only acceptable solution. I tap the metal tube.

Last night, my man-crazy roommate was giggling over the new guy in three-eleven north. The previous occupant was a gray-haired, bowtie-wearing tax auditor, his luxurious accommodations supplied by Nicolas. The most exciting thing he ever did was drink his tea on the balcony.

According to Cyndi, the new occupant is a delicious piece of man candy—tattooed, buff, and head-to-toe lickable. He was completing armcurls outside, and she enthusiastically counted his reps, oohing and aahing over his bulging biceps, calling to me to take a look.

I resisted that temptation, focusing on making macaroni and cheese for the two of us, the recipe snagged from the diner my mom works in. After we scarfed down dinner, Cyndi licking her plate clean, she left for the club and hasn't returned.

Three-eleven north is the mirror condo to ours. I

straighten the telescope. That position looks about right, but then, the imitation UGGs I bought in my second year of college looked about right also. The first time I wore the boots in the rain, the sheepskin fell apart, leaving me barefoot in Economics 201.

Unwilling to risk Cyndi's friendship on "about right," I gaze through the eyepiece. The view consists of rippling golden planes, almost like . . .

Tanned skin pulled over defined abs.

I blink. It can't be. I take another look. A perfect pearl of perspiration clings to a puckered scar. The drop elongates more and more, stretching, snapping. It trickles downward, navigating the swells and valleys of a man's honed torso.

No. I straighten. This is wrong. I shouldn't watch our sexy neighbor as he stands on his balcony. If anyone catches me . . .

Parts 1 – 6 available now!

An Excerpt from

RETURN TO CLAN SINCLAIR
A Clan Sinclair Novella
by Karen Ranney

When Ceana Sinclair Mead married the youngest
son of an Irish duke, she never dreamed that
seven years later her beloved Peter would die.
Her three brothers-in-law think she should
be grateful to remain a proper widow. After
three years of this, she's ready to scream. She
escapes to Scotland, only to discover she's so
much more than just the Widow Mead.

In Scotland, Ceana crosses paths with Bruce
Preston, an American tasked with a dangerous
mission by her brother, Macrath. Bruce is too
attractive for her peace of mind, but she still
finds him fascinating. Their one night together
is more wonderful than Ceana could have
imagined, and she has never felt more alive.

The darkness was nearly absolute, leaving her no choice but to stretch her hands out on either side of her, fingertips brushing against the stone walls. The incline was steep, further necessitating she take her time. Yet at the back of her mind was the last image she had of Carlton, his bright impish grin turning to horror as he glanced down.

The passage abruptly ended in a mushroom-shaped cavern. This was the grotto she'd heard so much about, with its flue in the middle and its broad, wide window looking out over the beach and the sea. She raced to the window, hopped up on the sill nature had created over thousands of years and leaned out.

A naked man reached up, grabbed Carlton as he fell. After he lowered the boy to the sand, he turned and smiled at her.

Carlton was racing across the beach, glancing back once or twice to see if he was indeed free. The rope made of sheets was hanging limply from his window.

The naked man was standing there with hands on his hips, staring at her in full frontal glory.

She hadn't seen many naked men, the last being her husband. The image in front of her now was so startling she couldn't help but stare. A smile was dawning on the stranger's full lips, one matched by his intent brown eyes. No, not quite brown, were they? They were like the finest Scottish whiskey touched with sunlight.

Her gaze danced down his strong and corded neck to broad shoulders etched with muscle. His chest was broad and muscled as well, tapering down to a slim waist and hips.

Even semiflaccid, his manhood was quite impressive.

The longer she watched, the more impressive it became.

What on earth was a naked man doing on Macrath's beach?

To her utter chagrin, the stranger turned and presented his backside to her, glancing over his shoulder to see if she approved of the sight.

She withdrew from the window, cheeks flaming. What on earth had she been doing? Who was she to gawk at a naked man as if she'd never before seen one?

Now that she knew Carlton was going to survive his escape, she should retreat immediately to the library.

"You'd better tell Alistair his brother's gotten loose again. Are you the new governess?"

She turned to find him standing in the doorway, still naked.

She pressed her fingers against the base of her throat and counseled herself to appear unaffected.

"I warn you, the imp escapes at any chance. You'll have your hands full there."

The look of fright on Carlton's face hadn't been fear of the distance to the beach, but the fact that he'd been caught.

She couldn't quite place the man's accent, but it wasn't Scottish. American, perhaps. What did she care where he came from? The problem was what he was doing here.

"I'm not a governess," she said. "I'm Macrath's sister, Ceana."

He bent and retrieved his shirt from a pile of clothes beside the door, taking his time with it. Shouldn't he have begun with his trousers instead?

"Who are you?" she asked, looking away as he began to don the rest of his clothing.

She'd had two children. She was well versed in matters of nature. She knew quite well what a man's body looked like. The fact that his struck her as singularly attractive was no doubt due to the fact she'd been a widow for three years.

"Well, Ceana Sinclair, is it all that important you know who I am?"

"It isn't Sinclair," she said. "It's Mead."

He tilted his head and studied her.

"Is Mr. Mead visiting along with you?"

She stared down at her dress of unremitting black. "I'm a widow," she said.

A shadow flitted over his face "Are you? Did Macrath know you were coming?"

"No," she said. "Does it matter? He's my brother. He's family. And why would you be wanting to know?"

He shrugged, finished buttoning his pants and began to don his shoes.

"Who are you?" she asked again.

"I'm a detective," he said. "My company was hired by your brother."

"Why?"

"Now that's something I'm most assuredly not going to tell you," he said. "It was nice meeting you, Mrs. Mead. I hope to see more of you before I leave."

And she hoped to see much, much less of him.

An Excerpt from

RETURN OF THE BAD GIRL
by *Codi Gary*

When Caroline Willis learns that her perfect
apartment has been double-booked—to a
dangerously hot bad boy—her bad-girl reputation
comes out in full force. But as close quarters
begin to ignite the sizzling chemistry between
them, she's left wondering: Bad boy plus bad
girl equals nothing but trouble . . . right?

"I feel like you keep looking for something more to me, but what you know about me is it. There's no 'deep down,' no mistaking my true character. I am bad news." He waited, listening for the tap of her retreating feet or the slam of the door, but only silence met his ears, then the soft sound of shoes on the cement floor—getting closer to him instead of farther away.

Fingers trailed feather-light touches over his lower back. "This scar on your back—is that from the accident?"

Her caress made his skin tingle as he shook his head. "I was knocked down by one of my mother's boyfriends and landed on a glass table."

"What about here?" Her hand had moved onto his right shoulder.

"It was a tattoo I had removed. In prison, you're safer if you belong, so—"

"I understand," she said, cutting him off. Had she heard the pain in his voice, or did she really understand?

He turned around before she could point out any more scars. "What are you doing?"

She looked him in the eye and touched the side of his neck, where his tattoo began, spreading all the way down past his shoulder and over his chest. "You say you're damaged. That you're bad news and won't ever change."

"Yeah?"

To his surprise, she dropped her hand to his and brought it up to her collarbone, where his finger felt a rough, puckered line.

"This is a knife wound—just a scratch, really—that I got from a man who used to come see me dance at the strip club. He was constantly asking me out, and I always let him down easy. But one night, after I'd had a shitty day, I told him I would never go out with an old, ugly fuck like him. He was waiting by my car when I got off work."

His rage blazed at this phantom from her past. "What happened?"

"I pulled a move I'd learned from one of the bouncers. Even though he still cut me, I was able to pick up a handful of gravel and throw it in his face. I made it to the front door of the club, and he took off. They arrested him on assault charges, and it turned out he had an outstanding warrant. I never saw him again."

Caroline pulled him closer, lifting her arm for him to see a jagged scar along her forearm. "This is from a broken beer bottle I got sliced with when a woman came into my bar in San Antonio, looking for her husband. She didn't take it well when she found out he had a girlfriend on the side, and when I stepped in to stop her from attacking him, she sliced me."

He couldn't stop his hand from sliding up over her soft skin until it rested on the back of her neck, his fingers pressing into her flesh until she tilted her chin up to meet his gaze.

"What's your point with all the show-and-tell, Caroline?"

She reached out and smoothed his chest with her hand. "I don't care how damaged you are, because I am just as broken, maybe more so."

Her words tore at him, twisting him up inside as his other hand cupped the back of her head. "You don't want to go here with me, princess. I'm only going to break your heart."

The laugh that passed those beautiful lips was bitter and sad. "Trust me, my heart was shattered long before I ever met you."

Gabe wanted her, wanted to believe that he could find comfort in her body without the complications that would inevitably come, but he'd seen her heart firsthand. She had one. It might be wrapped up in a mile-thick layer of cowhide, but a part of Caroline Willis was still open to new emotions. New love.

And he wasn't.

But he wanted to kiss her anyway.

He dropped his head until his lips hovered above hers, and he watched as they parted when he came closer. Her hot breath teased his mouth, and he couldn't stop while she was warm and willing. He might not get another chance to taste her, and while a better man would have walked away, he wasn't that guy.